THE LAST BUFFALO

An invasion of reformers and prohibitionists has led to the gradual disappearance of the big herds of buffalo from the Great Plains. In Sulphur Creek, the saloon owners have hired gunslingers to intimidate these newcomers, and young Jock Sumner is caught right in the middle. As a ward of the town marshal, Sumner is hot property. And when a hunter named O'Brien learns that the boy and the town are in trouble, he decides that it is up to him to prevent a war from tearing the town apart . . .

Books by Ralph Hayes
in the Linford Western Library:

THE TOMBSTONE VENDETTA
FORT REVENGE

RALPH HAYES

THE LAST BUFFALO

Complete and Unabridged

LINFORD
Leicester

First published in Great Britain in 2013 by
Robert Hale Limited
London

First Linford Edition
published 2014
by arrangement with
Robert Hale Limited
London

A catalogue record for this book is available
from the British Library.

ISBN 978–1–4448–2139–0

Published by
F. A. Thorpe (Publishing)
Anstey, Leicestershire

Set by Words & Graphics Ltd.
Anstey, Leicestershire
Printed and bound in Great Britain by
T. J. International Ltd., Padstow, Cornwall

This book is printed on acid-free paper

1

It was a typical hell-raising Saturday night in Sulphur Creek, Kansas.

Drunken cowpokes and drifters were racing their ponies up and down Main Street, firing six-shooters into the blackness overhead, and shouting profanities at the night. In early evening a trail bum had been shot dead in the street by persons unknown, and Marshal Uriah Tate was still busy looking for witnesses, but without success.

In the Prairie Schooner saloon, ranch hands, gamblers and gunslingers stood along the mahogany bar or sat red-eyed at tables, sidearms displayed ostentatiously on their hips. A gray-haired woman stood near the front of the crowded room, addressing the unmindful patrons futilely, her voice lost in the din of noise from wild-looking drinkers and a tinny piano at the rear. A

1

Women's Christian Temperance Union patch was sewn on the breast of her gingham dress; she was one of a small cadre of reformers who had descended on Sulphur Creek and Kansas in recent weeks. The movement had already enjoyed some success in Dodge City and Wichita, and now its local activists were hoping for a similar result here in this back-country cowtown.

'The road to Hell is paved with your liquor bottles, gentlemen!' the WCTU woman cried out above the noise. 'You must abstain from the Devil's brew, and quit this dwelling place of demons!'

She droned on and nobody listened. At a table not far away three men sat, playing stud poker. They were hired guns employed by the saloon owner Luke Mallory to intimidate the rather aggressive National Prohibition Movement group, some of whom were advocating the closure of saloons altogether.

'*Caramba*! Luck is my lady tonight, *compadres*,' one of the three gunmen yelled, raking in a big pot of silver and bills. He was Pedro Rueda, who had just been passing through town when Mallory had hired him. He was a tough-looking Mexican immigrant who had once met the Apache chief Geronimo, and was wanted for multiple murders in his own country. He had a black mustache and very dark hair underneath a black hat adorned with silver buttons along its band. 'Hey, let me buy you losers a round of drinks, sí?' He had been the heavy drinker of them. '*Hola*, Betty! One more bottle of that Planter's Rye, *por favor*! *Rapido*, my little *putita*!'

He was addressing a blonde, buxom saloon girl called Big Betty. She and her co-hostess, Nita Ruiz, were the current targets of the reformers, because of their upstairs activities with patrons, and Mallory had already been warned to get rid of them. Betty gave him a sour look. 'Keep your pants on, wetback. And remember. Cash on delivery.'

Rueda made kissing sounds with his lips. Across the table from him a tall, slim fellow sat eyeing Rueda glumly. He was R.C. Wilson, one of the fastest guns in the state, and he didn't really like this Hispanic hire of Mallory's. Next to him was an albino called 'Rabbit' Purcell, whom Wilson had brought with him when Mallory hired Wilson. Everybody shied away from Purcell because of his strange look, except for Wilson. Purcell had killed his own brother in a gunfight in Laredo, and was dangerous because of his quick temper.

Purcell was also staring hard at Rueda. 'How do you keep doing that without cheating, Mex?' he growled out in a menacing tone.

Rueda frowned through a grin. 'Cheat? I don't have to cheat to beat a lousy player like you, *Blancito*.'

Purcell had pink eyes, white, straw-like hair, and a pallid skin. But his pale face turned the hue of his irises now. 'You saying I can't play poker, you Mexican poultry thief!'

Now Rueda was angry, too. But Wilson intervened. 'All right, you two. Maybe we better put the cards away for a while. The noise in here is getting on our nerves.'

Rueda hesitated, then nodded. He gave Purcell a sober look, then turned toward the mahogany bar. 'Hey! How about that bottle, *muchacha*?'

'Put your trust in sobriety and the word of God!' the reform woman was shouting. Her name was Nell Douglas and she looked very tired. Usually a male reformer came with her on these forays.

Over behind the bar, standing beside his obese bartender, Luke Mallory glanced at Nell and shook his head slowly. If she were a man he could have thrown her out by now. He turned to Big Betty. 'Tell Rueda we're out of Planter's,' he said quietly. 'I think maybe he's had enough for the night, anyway.'

Big Betty leaned on the bar. 'I'd like to pour one on his head,' she grunted.

At the table of three, Purcell's irritation was diverted to Nell Douglas, who was now reading loudly from a prayer book. He slammed his hand down on to the table, and rose from his chair. 'Who let that Bible-thumper in here?' he roared out. His pink eyes were flashing fire.

'Take it easy, Rabbit,' Wilson said. He rarely became flustered about anything. He had stone-cold gray eyes, with a thin scar running across the left eye. Few men ventured to cross him, or even dispute with him. It was rumored that he had made John Wesley Hardin back off a showdown a couple of years ago in Laramie.

Rueda was grinning at Purcell's transplanted irritation. Purcell now strode unexpectedly over to Nell, who quit reading when she saw him coming. When he reached her he drew the Colt Army .45 on his hip and placed its muzzle up against her forehead.

'Take your damn Bible out of here or I'll blow the back of your head off,' he growled in a low, menacing tone.

Nell gasped, and backed away from the gun a half-step. 'I see the evil of Satan in those frightening eyes, sinner! But the hand of God will protect me from your debauchery!'

Purcell cocked the revolver, and suddenly all noise in the saloon subsided. 'Are you hard of hearing, lady?'

From behind the bar Luke Mallory shook his head. He had wondered whether he should accept this hot-headed sidekick of Wilson's just to have another gun available to him. Hank Logan, down the street at the Lost Dogie, had settled for one lone gunslinger. 'Rabbit! Put that gun away! I'll handle this!'

Purcell hurled a scalding look at Mallory, and violently reholstered the gun. Then he turned back to Nell, and jerked the prayer book from her grasp. He walked a few paces to the front entrance and threw the book out onto the street.

'Now. Go get your damn book, you ugly psalm-singing freak!'

Nell's lower lip quivered slightly. 'For shame, ravager of decency! Soon this haven of perfidy will be closed to you, and soulless half-men like you will have to satisfy their base habits elsewhere!'

Purcell's face turned hard again. 'What did you call me?'

'Rabbit. Let it go,' Wilson urged him quietly.

Outside on the street at that moment, a fifteen-year-old boy named Jock Sumner had just watched the prayer book land at his feet and had stopped to pick it up. He was a local ranch hand who was a friend and unofficial ward of Marshal Uriah Tate. He knew Nell Douglas well, and recognized the prayer book as hers. Looking up at the swinging doors of the saloon he listened to the quiet inside and wondered if Nell were in trouble. He hesitated just a moment, then climbed three steps and pushed through the doors and into the saloon.

Purcell was standing nose-to-nose with Nell, making her breathless with his menacing proximity. 'Now, tell me again what you just called me,' he growled.

Jock assessed the situation quickly. He had just come from the jail and knew Tate was on his way past the saloons shortly and, since Jock hadn't begun carrying a sidearm yet, he suddenly wished he had waited for Tate.

'Evening, Nell,' Jock said loudly and pleasantly. 'I thought I heard you in here. Maybe it's getting time to go home.' He was a rather tall boy, at just under six feet, and was nice-looking, with dark hair and eyes. He was the nephew of a deceased bounty hunter named Wesley Sumner, and now orphaned.

'Who the hell are you?' Purcell said angrily.

'That's the Sumner kid,' Mallory said from the bar. 'Our beloved marshal has taken him under his wing. Let him take her home.'

Everybody in the saloon was listening to the exchange now. 'No, no. Just a minute here,' Purcell said, frowning. 'Sumner. Ain't I heard that name before?'

'My uncle was Wesley 'Certainty' Sumner,' Jock said quietly.

Purcell's face changed, and he moved from Nell to Jock, staring hard at him. 'You mean that yellow weasel back-shooter that went after men for reward money?' he said in a low, chilling voice.

Wilson and Rueda were enjoying the show now. 'I met him once out in Albuquerque,' Wilson said to the Mexican. 'He was figuring to go after Bonney. But Masterson beat him to the Kid.'

Over near the doors, though, things were not so calm. Jock's face had colored at the insult to his dead uncle. 'My uncle Wesley was the bravest man I've ever known,' he said emotionally. 'And I think it's you, mister, that has a yellow streak up his back.'

He realized immediately he had gone

too far, but it was too late. Purcell moved up very close to him and threw a hard fist into Jock's face. The blow was heard across the room and Jock went flying against the wall behind him, then slid to the floor, dazed. He spat out some blood.

'You sonofabitch!' he blurted out.

Purcell drew the Colt again, and leveled it at Jock's chest. 'Nobody's ever called me yellow and lived to tell it,' he hissed out.

'Rabbit! Hold it!' Wilson called to him. 'He's just a stupid kid.'

'I don't care if he's St Peter,' Purcell spat out. 'So long, kid.'

Jock thought it was all over. There was a muffled scream from Nell, and then the swinging doors pushed open and Marshal Tate stood there.

Tate was middle-aged with a barrel chest and bowed legs, and he was no gunfighter. But he wore a badge and did his best to stand up to those who were good with guns. He saw Jock on the floor and the gun in Purcell's hand.

'What the hell is going on here?' he said carefully.

Purcell glanced at him with little concern. 'I'm going to blow this kid's liver out through his back,' he said in a tight voice.

Tate laid his hand on the Colt Navy revolver on his belt. 'I'd advise against that, Purcell,' he said evenly.

Purcell turned the gun on him. 'Is that right, Marshal?'

'Damn it, Purcell!' Mallory called out.

'Put it away, Rabbit,' Wilson said from the table.

Purcell whirled toward him. 'Who says?'

Wilson sighed heavily. 'I say.' He held Purcell's gaze with an ice-cold one. Purcell hesitated a moment, then turned and fired his Colt raucously into the ceiling, making Nell jump. He gave Jock a long, burning look, and holstered his weapon. He walked over to the bar. 'Give me a drink. Now!' he barked out.

Jock was picking himself up off the

floor. He touched his face where blood stained his mouth and chin.

'Are you OK?' Tate asked him.

Jock nodded.

'Then maybe you better get Nell on home,' the marshal said quietly. He turned to Nell, who looked pale. 'And you ought to stay out of here for a spell,' he added. 'I'll look in on you two later.'

Jock's anger was still burgeoning inside his chest. He took a deep breath in. 'OK, Uriah.'

A moment later they were gone, with Purcell casting a deadly look after them, from where he stood at the bar. Tate walked over to him. 'What kind of man are you? To knock a boy down like that?'

Purcell turned arrogantly toward him. 'The kid's got a foul mouth. A lot like that no-good uncle of his used to have.'

'Well, I'll talk to him. He might want to file charges.'

Purcell laughed in his throat. 'Don't

worry, Marshal. That will all be taken care of.'

Tate frowned at him. 'What does that mean?'

'You're the law. You figure it out.'

'Why don't you bring that drink over here, Rabbit?' Wilson called out to him.

'A good idea,' Luke Mallory said quickly. His bartender, standing a few feet away, wiped sweat off his face. The room remained silent.

Purcell grinned crookedly at Tate, and carried his drink over to the table where Wilson and Rueda still sat. Big Betty, standing at the bar a short distance away, came over toward Tate. 'Nice seeing you again, Marshal. Why don't you have a drink with us?'

'I've got a nice little Cognac here that might tickle your palate,' Mallory told him, smiling easily. Since Tate had given the reformers some legitimacy by attending a couple of their meetings, and had acceded to their compromise demand of removing saloon prostitutes from the Prairie Schooner and Lost

Dogie, he had become an adversary in the minds of the saloon owners.

'I didn't come in here to drink,' Tate said soberly. 'It looked like an innocent woman and boy was getting themselves in trouble here.'

'That's just it, Marshal,' Wilson spoke up. Purcell had rejoined them at the table now. 'They got themselves in trouble. That woman is an irritation to every honest patron in this room.'

'That's right!' a drunk cowhand called out from a nearby table. 'And now you're doing the same thing, Tate!'

Tate ignored the outburst and walked over to Wilson's table. He hated these gunslingers the saloon men had brought in, and figured their type could end up causing a shooting war with the reformers.

'Sounds like you might have seen the whole thing, Wilson.'

'That's right,' Wilson said pleasantly. He sat tall on his chair, an Enfield Mark II revolver hanging wicked-looking from his side. 'The boy came in here looking for trouble, Marshal. Throwing insults around. Acting cocky. Rabbit here thought the kid was going to throw a punch, and beat him to it. And that's all of it. Right, Pedro?'

'*Sí, exacto!*' Rueda said loudly. 'I saw everything, Marshal.'

'Well, why don't we get that all down in writing?' Tate said. 'You boys can walk down to the office with me, and I'll get statements from both of you.'

The room became even more hushed. Wilson looked up at Tate with an insolent gaze. 'Now why would we want to go to all that bother, Marshal?'

Tate grunted out a short laugh. 'That's what I thought.' He turned to the other patrons. 'If anybody saw what really happened, stop in at the jail and I'll take signed statements from you.'

'Get to hell out of here, Marshal!' somebody yelled from down the long bar.

Purcell stood up somberly. 'Anybody signs a statement against me will, by

God, answer to me!'

Tate turned back to him. 'That's interference with the law, Purcell.'

'So?' Purcell said hotly.

Tate just stood there, uncertain. He and everyone in the room knew he couldn't stand up against Mallory's hired guns. Not even with his inept deputy Webster at his side. 'Just keep them remarks to yourself,' he said in a more subdued tone.

'You're still welcome to that drink, Marshal,' Luke Mallory called to him.

Tate was glad for the excuse to retreat from the gunfighters' table. He walked over to the mahogany bar and Big Betty.

'Why is she still here, Luke?' he said, looking at her.

The buxom blonde shrugged. 'Why not?'

'Where's Nita Ruiz?' Tate added. 'Is she here somewhere too?'

'She's upstairs with a customer,' Betty said with a grin. 'Sewing a patch on his trousers.'

Laughter from the room.

'We're discussing your offer,' Mallory said. 'Even if they leave, they would have to have notice. We try to treat employees with fairness, Uriah.'

'This was supposed to be a done deal,' Tate said. 'To make them people down at the NPM stop talking about saloon closures.'

Mallory smiled. 'We're not worried about saloon closures.'

Tate sighed. 'Look, Luke. I shouldn't have to remind you that Kansas is a dry state now. Saloons are open in Dodge and other towns at the indulgence of the local law.'

'And the citizenry,' Mallory added.

Tate shrugged. 'The point is, be content with a compromise.'

A ranch hand nearby spoke up. 'How come you ain't hassling Rosie down at the Lost Dogie?' he called out. 'Could it be because Mayor Provost visits her twice a week?'

The ranch man and several others burst out in laughter, and once again

Tate ignored the outburst.

'All the girls will have to go, Luke,' he said quietly. 'And I'm going to have to take action on this real soon. I'll be back.'

Purcell turned on his chair to face Tate. 'Why don't you go arrest that yellow dog out yonder for pissing in the street, Marshal?' he muttered in a low, grating tone. He was still seething over young Jock Sumner.

Tate walked past him on his way out. 'I'm going to talk with Jock about this incident, Purcell.'

'Talk with him all you want,' Purcell said. 'I'm good with that.'

Tate studied those pink eyes for a moment and didn't like what he saw there. He turned then, and left without further comment.

When he was gone Purcell turned to Wilson. 'Don't get in my way on this. When I catch that kid alone some dark night, he's dead.'

Wilson didn't bother trying to dissuade him. When Purcell got into one of his crazy moods about something, discussion was pointless.

★ ★ ★

The next day, far to the north of Kansas, it was one of those pristine early-spring mornings in the mountains of upper Colorado, with wildflower blossoms punching up through scattered patches of snow, and mule deer tracks deep in the soft mud. At a small, icy stream at the bottom edge of the high country, a hunter named O'Brien knelt just inches from the gurgling creek and unloaded a dead ermine from a steel trap.

'I'll be damned,' he muttered with satisfaction, looking the animal over. Ermine pelts brought big money at the trappers' rendezvous at Missoula. He had expected only beaver along this creek.

He removed a long Bowie hunting knife from a scabbard on his right stovepipe boot and began carefully skinning his prize. He was a big, athletic-looking man, with long, shaggy hair and a thick but short mustache. He wore a coat of beaver pelts over rawhides, and a dark-stained Stetson on his head. There was no sidearm on his belt, but he carried two rifles on his Appaloosa's irons. The horse was picketed to a scraggly bush fifty yards away, on higher ground.

O'Brien looked up from the skinning and stared toward a stand of aspens not twenty yards away, where he had heard an almost indiscernible noise.

He listened intently, his dark blue eyes squinting down as he let the light breeze fill his nostrils. He glanced toward the Appaloosa, and the horse guttered quietly. He stared some more, then went back to his work. He was wide-shouldered and muscular, with a wind-tanned, weathered face, and he worked now with thick, bare hands on the ermine, taking the pelt and meat quickly and skilfully. He had been perhaps the most successful of the

Northern Plains buffalo hunters, but now the herds had thinned out so badly with the big hide companies going after them that he had had to do a lot of trapping to survive. He was now holed up in an abandoned mountain cabin just a few miles from this stream, and had been there through the winter.

O'Brien was just over forty; his rugged features had lost some of their youthful look and there was a hint of gray in his unkempt hair. But he was just as physical as he had ever been, and just as dangerous to any man who gave him trouble.

When he had finished with the ermine he heard the sound again, a slight rustling from the tree line, and now the picketed horse was acting anxious. This time the hunter rose slowly and scented the air again, then furrowed his brow. Yes, it was bear.

He had known there was a grizzly hereabouts, a monster that was reputed to have killed two other trappers without provocation, just because they were operating in his territory. The Appaloosa was now straining at the picket line, and O'Brien figured the bear to be between himself and his mount, on whose flanks two long guns hung useless. Both O'Brien and the Appaloosa were in danger.

He had taken just three steps toward the horse when the big bear emerged from the trees. It stared right at O'Brien, and then glanced at the horse, which now whinnied loudly, broke its tether, and ran off into the trees with the rifles.

O'Brien dropped the ermine pelt and stood there motionless. The last time he had had to kill a grizzly, a couple of years ago, he had shot it with a Sharps .500 buffalo gun. His only weapons now were his skinning knife and his bare hands.

The bear, just fifteen yards away, rose up on its hind legs and roared so loudly that O'Brien could feel vibrations in his chest. The bear intended to kill him. There was no way to outrun or out-climb the animal. O'Brien had to stand and fight.

The grizzly was back on all fours and coming at him. It came almost casually, making dark rumblings in its throat. O'Brien reached down, picked up a three-foot-long dead branch and held it out in front of him, the Bowie in his other hand. The bear snarled and kept coming.

O'Brien circled quickly to his left, making the animal slow down and adjust the direction of its attack. He could already smell the iron stink of the bear in his nostrils now, and see the slather in its open maw. Small, coal-ember eyes burned in a fierce face. Its claws were four inches long. It rose again onto its hind legs and threw itself at him.

The makeshift club was torn from O'Brien's grasp in a split second as the animal knocked him to the ground, its full weight crashing onto him like a freight wagon. A long claw ripped at his shoulder, tearing at flesh. The snarling mouth was in his face, the hot, rancid breath enveloping him. Teeth were bared, as big as pocket knives, ready to tear O'Brien's head off his shoulders.

It was now or never. His right arm slid free from the powerful leg beside his chest, and with all his strength he thrust the Bowie up to the hilt into the bear's heart.

The grizzly stopped snarling, not quite understanding what had happened to it yet. Its jaw worked once, twice, then it fell full length with a ground-shaking thud onto O'Brien's supine form. Its muzzle was in his face, the eyes slowly glazing over. The beast's forelegs embraced him. The enormous body gave one huge shudder from head to toe, then lay motionless.

O'Brien could hardly breathe. 'You mangy, motherless bastard,' he grunted out, trying to pull air into his lungs.

He had to just lie there for a while, waiting for his strength to come back. It took a half-hour after that to crawl free of the enormous corpse. O'Brien struggled to his feet, covered with blood. He took one step and fell back to the ground. He muttered several obscenities, tried again, and succeeded. He had lost his hat and his wild hair was in his face. His beaver coat was ruined but it had helped save his life. His rawhide shirt was stained with his blood from the gash on his left shoulder. His left leg was scraped and cut, and one of his boots lay ten feet away in high weeds. He had a claw wound across his right cheek, which would leave a permanent scar, and his body was so bruised he felt like he had been run over by an over-sized conestoga.

He kicked the bear savagely in its ribs; it made a spasmic movement and he stepped back from it. His immigrant Scottish father, back in Tennessee, had told him early on that you can't presume a bear is dead till you've got it skinned and the hide tanned. But this one seemed pretty dead now.

He knelt unsteadily over the bear and examined the pelt. It would bring a good price at the nearest market. He went after the Appaloosa then, and found it grazing along the creek a hundred yards downstream. The horse was glad to see him.

'Next time you run off with my guns, take the damn bear with you,' O'Brien greeted it. It guffered quietly in response. 'Yeah, it's OK. He can't hurt us no more.'

When he got the horse back to the bear it balked and reared for a moment as it got wind of the dead animal. O'Brien picketed the horse to a nearby cottonwood tree, removed the torn-up beaver coat, and began skinning the bear. Over an hour later he had the pelt laid out on the ground and had cut off some steaks, which he took over to a skin bag on his saddle. When he reached into a saddle-bag for a cloth to wash his face at the stream his hand fell upon a folded page. He pulled it out. It was a letter he had received from Jock Sumner a couple weeks ago, when he visited his post office box in Fort Collins.

'Hell,' he mumbled when he saw he had stained it with blood and bear fat. He stuffed it back into the bag.

O'Brien had ridden with a bounty hunter called Certainty Sumner for a brief time a few years back, and they had formed a rare friendship. Before Sumner had been killed by outlaws, he had mentioned Jock, his nephew, as his only surviving relative. So when O'Brien had passed through Sulphur Creek a year ago he felt he owed it to Sumner to meet Jock and answer any questions he had about his deceased uncle.

O'Brien went down to the creek and washed his face and hands. The morning had warmed up some and he was glad to be rid of the coat. Squatting there by the gurgling water, he recalled that lone meeting with the boy. Jock had talked O'Brien's ear off, and O'Brien had taken him out on the range, let him set up the Sharps buffalo gun and fire it. This was the third letter that Jock had written; it was all about how bad things were getting in Sulphur Creek, with a shooting war looming between the newly arrived reformers and the saloon owners.

The Appaloosa shied at receiving the big pelt, but then O'Brien was aboard and glad to be heading back to the cabin.

It had been an eventful outing.

★ ★ ★

At about the same time, two riders halted fifty yards downhill from O'Brien's cabin. They studied it for a long moment. The bigger of them wore a badge on his coat, and his name was Logan. He was a recently appointed marshal in a small village thirty miles to the east, the nearest point of civilization to the cabin. His companion was a thin, emaciated-looking fellow, a drinking companion of Logan, whose name was Weeks. Logan was an ex-outlaw who extorted money from local businesses and bullied the citizens, spending most of his time drinking and gambling. His village council was getting ready to fire him, but he didn't know that yet.

It made Weeks feel important to be allowed to accompany the town marshal, and he expected Logan to appoint him his deputy one day soon. Logan, though, had no such intention.

'Well, looky here,' Weeks commented as they eyed the cabin. 'Looks like this old trapper's hut is being used. Must be one of them mountain men. Live like hogs and smell like cow dung.' He gave a high cackle of a laugh.

Logan nodded. He was broad-coupled and husky-looking, wearing a thick wool coat and a small-brimmed hat. 'They do tend to stink up a room when they come in. Looks like this one might be out checking his traps. Although I see a pack animal tethered at the rear there.'

'Maybe we better have us a look inside,' Weeks suggested eagerly.

They rode on up to the front of the

cabin and dismounted. The cabin was a small structure, built into a hillside with a sod roof. It was well protected from the harsh winters, though. They walked up to the door, which was hung on leather straps. Logan pushed the door open warily, his hand on a .44 revolver on a thick belt. They both entered, looking around.

Sun slanted in from the doorway behind them, and from a small, translucent hide window set in one wall. Logan looked around sourly. There was a guttering-out fire in a fireplace set in another wall. There was a table and a chair, and a cot in a far corner.

'Hey, look what we got over here!' Weeks exclaimed happily.

They walked over to a stack of pelts in another corner, all cured and ready for market. Logan lifted some by their edges and whistled softly. 'This boy must be good. I never seen such a bunch of high-quality hides.'

Weeks's eyes were big. 'Them would

bring plenty on the Fort Collins market.'

Logan nodded. 'Even more than you think. Seems a shame to leave all this to some seedy hide man, don't it?'

Weeks grinned inanely. 'I was hoping you'd say that, Marshal.'

'I reckon we could get these all loaded onto the rumps of our own mounts, without bothering with that packhorse out there. Ride them into town and sell them off before he even knows they're gone. Hell, if he comes looking, I'll throw his butt in jail.'

Weeks laughed and slapped his thigh. 'By God, we got ourselves a damn treasure trove!'

'You start carrying these pelts outside. I'll just nose around and see if he might have some gold or silver stashed away in here.'

Weeks's rheumy eyes had a new glitter in them. 'What do you think they'll bring? Shouldn't we take them on over to Fort Collins for the best price?'

Logan dropped a hard look on the other man. He had little interest in sharing this windfall with Weeks. 'Just get on with getting them all outside. We want to be clear of here as soon as . . .'

They both turned toward the open doorway as the sound of another horse came to them from outside. It was O'Brien, returning on the Appaloosa, stiff and sore from the mauling by the grizzly. He had slowed his approach when he saw the two mounts picketed outside the cabin.

'The trapper! He's back!' Weeks said breathlessly.

Logan squinted into the sun, and got a glimpse of O'Brien, who had reined in his mount and was studying the two other horses. 'Don't worry. This don't change nothing. Let me handle it,' said Logan in a calm voice.

Out in the sun, O'Brien dismounted from the stallion, slid his Winchester from its saddle scabbard, and strode slowly to the doorway. He figured some travelers must be helping themselves to his coffee, which was permissible. Then he stood in the entrance, his big frame filling the opening ominously.

'Who the hell are you two?' he growled at them.

Weeks swallowed hard when he saw the wild, primitive look of the man, made more dramatic by the signs of O'Brien's morning ordeal. Weeks's right hand inched closer to an old, single-shot pistol hanging on his thigh.

O'Brien had already spotted the undisturbed pot of coffee and the disturbed pile of hides in the corner. Logan stepped forward, letting the sunlight fall on to his badge. 'Morning, stranger. I'm Marshal Logan from Birney Pass. You must know the place. We saw your door ajar and stopped to make sure everything was OK here. You look kind of beat up, mister. You in need of medical attention?'

O'Brien had seen the badge, and relaxed. He came on in, and looked the two visitors over more carefully. 'I'm fine,' he said. 'It was just some damn bear.' He leaned the Winchester against the fireplace stones. 'You're welcome to my coffee. You out hunting?'

Logan forced a smile. 'Just trying to find us some quail for supper. But I see you been having better luck.' He nodded toward the pelts.

'That's a whole winter of trapping,' O'Brien told him. He poured himself a cup of cold coffee, and hung a pot over the low embers of the fire. He sipped the coffee and noticed for the first time the tension now showing in Weeks's face.

Logan was relaxed, though, now that O'Brien was disarmed. He sat near him on the edge of the crude table. 'All winter or not, that's a lot of pelts you got piled up back there.'

O'Brien narrowed his piercing blue eyes on to him. 'They ain't for sale. I already got a buyer at Fort Collins.'

Logan looked O'Brien over. 'Buying wasn't what I had in mind. I was wondering whether you trapped all them furs yourself, mister.'

O'Brien was becoming irritated very quickly. He had had a bad morning. 'What the hell are you trying to say, Marshal?' He felt a stab of pain slice through his left shoulder, from the bear attack.

Logan arched his brow. 'We got reports from area Indians, reporting theft from their traps. You sure some of them skins didn't come into your possession illegally, mister?' His manner was quiet, easy.

O'Brien's face hardened even more, and the look on it made a chill crawl down Weeks's spine. 'Is that an accusation?' O'Brien responded.

Logan remained calm. 'I'm just saying. Maybe I better show these pelts to some other trappers and area Indians. To see if they make any claim on them. Nothing personal, you understand. It's just my job. You could probably get them back later. Through a legal process.'

O'Brien still held the cup of coffee. When he had poured it, he had set the pot on the low fire and kicked the flame up a bit. Now he emptied his cup out, and poured a fresh cup of hot coffee before he answered Logan.

'I trapped all them pelts myself, Marshal. And you ain't taking them anywhere.' He was standing near the Winchester, but realized a move toward it would be dangerous.

Logan was actually pleased with O'Brien's reaction. If the trapper gave him trouble, he could kill him without remorse and claim self-defense if the story ever got out. He reached casually to his hip and drew his gun. Seeing the move, Weeks excitedly drew his own pistol.

'That saucy manner will get you a gut full of lead!' he barked out.

'Shut up, Weeks,' Logan said levelly.

'Huh?'

'You're beginning to act like a guilty man,' Logan said to O'Brien. 'You got any gold hid away in here, from your ill-gotten gains?'

O'Brien sighed. 'You really want to

do this, Logan? Why don't you just let it go?'

Logan laughed quietly. 'Weeks. Go get that Winchester.'

Weeks glanced at him and realized that Logan intended to question his prisoner in his own special way. He grinned and headed past O'Brien toward the long gun.

'Where do you think you're going?' came O'Brien's deep voice.

Weeks stopped in front of the buffalo hunter. 'I'm confiscating that rifle over there, Rawhide.' But a fine dew of sweat had popped out on his upper lip, betraying the tension under the bravado. His close proximity to this wild-looking man made him nervous. 'You got any idea about stopping me?'

He had just reholstered the one-shot pistol in preparation for retrieving the Winchester, but felt safe with Logan's revolver leveled at O'Brien's chest. In that moment after his response, he almost reached for the old weapon again.

'Nobody handles that Winchester but

me, flea-brain,' O'Brien said.

Weeks started breathing shallowly. 'Shoot him!' he yelled over his shoulder at Logan, feeling the hair prickle up at the back of his neck. Then he went for his own gun.

While his hand was still on its way to his holster, O'Brien threw his cup of hot coffee into his face.

The hot liquid hit Weeks's eyes and blinded him momentarily. Then he was screaming in pain, grabbing at his face. Logan was off the table and aiming at O'Brien, but Weeks was in his line of sight.

'Weeks, get away, damn it!' Logan was yelling.

O'Brien raised his right, uninjured leg, planted it on Weeks's midsection, and kicked out hard. Weeks went flying away as if shot from a catapult, quick-stepping backwards and crashing into Logan and the table, taking both down with him as he flew past, his lower ribs fractured from the impact of the savage kick.

Logan swore as Weeks hit him, and as he went down he squeezed off two rounds at O'Brien. The first one burned a flesh wound over O'Brien's ribcage, the next one missed his head by a fraction of an inch, as he dived toward the rifle and the floor. He grabbed the gun as he fell past it, and found its trigger assembly as he hit the floor beside the fireplace.

Weeks was groaning on the floor behind Logan, and reaching for the pistol again. Logan's scowl had a hint of fear in it now, as he aimed and fired again, but too hastily. The hot lead chewed up fireplace stone beside O'Brien's shoulder and propelled a chunk against O'Brien's jaw; it stung like a bullet. Then O'Brien, still lying on his back, fired the Winchester twice from the hip and hit Logan high in the chest and in the right eye.

Logan went hurtling wildly, crashed over the overturned table and landed beside Weeks, who had his pistol ready to fire now. Weeks glanced wide-eyed at

Logan for a moment, then made a fatal mistake. Instead of throwing the gun down, he panicked and aimed to fire. O'Brien fired the long gun a third time, and hit Weeks in mid-chest. The lead exploded his heart and blew out a posterior rib as he fell on to his back again, shuddered once, and was still.

O'Brien pulled himself up to a sitting position for a moment, and just stared at the two would-be thieves. Of all the injuries he had suffered through this long morning, the one he noticed most at the moment was the stinging on his jaw from the chip of concrete. He thought about that as he sat there, and grinned slightly.

'And it ain't even noon yet,' he grumbled under his breath.

After a few minutes he pulled himself to his feet. The acrid gunsmoke had drifted out of the cabin, and the air was good to breathe again. He walked over to the two intruders and saw they were both very dead.

'Was a few beaver skins worth this,

you nitwits?' he asked the corpses.

Outside, the Appaloosa nickered quietly.

'Yeah, I'm all right,' O'Brien called back tiredly.

He righted the table and chair, laid the Winchester down, and without looking at the lifeless figures again, went back outside to get the bear meat and pelts out of the direct sun, and to unsaddle the Appaloosa and picket it behind the cabin with his packhorse. He then went inside, stepped over the corpses and heated up some stew. Then he had a light meal as he worked.

In early afternoon he buried the two failed robbers with their saddles up in the woods behind the cabin, and released their horses into the mountains. Then he scraped his pelts clean ready for curing in the sun.

He had been thinking about moving on, even before this morning's incidents. The trapping would be worse here for a few seasons. And now there was the situation of a dead lawman. The mounts would probably wind up in Birney Pass eventually, and would be recognized. If people came looking this way, it would be best if he was gone.

He had had the notion for some time of returning to the Oklahoma Territory for some trapping, and hoping to run into one of the rare buffalo herds on the way. He hadn't taken a buff pelt in over six months, and they used to be so thick on the plains that a man could ride through a herd all morning without coming to the far side of it. But winds of change were sweeping the West. A man had to change with them, or perish.

Sitting at his table in the cabin that evening, he decided. He would take his pelts to Fort Collins, sell them and his pack-horse, and head south. He took out Jock Sumner's bloodstained letter and scanned it slowly. He was a very poor reader, but could make out the sense of it. The kid talked about those same winds of change in Sulphur Creek, blown in by the reform movement. And O'Brien felt there was

43

something else in the letter hidden between the lines. Behind the casual reporting O'Brien sensed a subtle fear.

Maybe he would stop in at Sulphur Creek on his way to the Territory. Have another good talk with his old friend's nephew. Make sure everything was all right with him. Let him shoot the buffalo gun again.

Yes, he would leave just as soon as he could clear the cabin out.

It might be just the kind of change he needed now in his life.

2

A couple of days had passed since the incident with Jock Sumner and Nell Douglas at the Prairie Schooner saloon. Jock had decided it would be pointless to file charges against Rabbit Purcell, and Marshal Tate had agreed. Tate had returned to the saloon, however, and reported to Luke Mallory that the reform group chairman, Avery Hawkins, had visited Tate at his office with two other NPM members and demanded immediate firing of all saloon girls, or there would be 'consequences'. Mallory had laughed at the threat, and Tate had left steaming with anger, but had taken no precipitate action yet against the saloons. But he had heard that one NPM hot-head, a fellow named Will St Clair, had hinted that one solution to all this would be to burn the saloons to the ground.

Things were heating up.

At the end of that second day, Tate had left his deputy Webster in charge at the jail, and ridden home to his cabin at the south end of town. He hadn't been there for a half-hour when Jock Sumner knocked on his door.

'Jock! What a nice surprise! I thought you'd be sleeping out at the ranch tonight.' Jock had lived with a grandmother until a year ago, when she died of pneumonia in a bad winter. Now Jock had no living relatives. Tate had gotten him a job at a local ranch, and had befriended the boy. Jock often stayed over at Tate's cabin on weekends, instead of sleeping in the ranch bunkhouse.

Jock removed a sheepskin jacket and sat down at Tate's table with him. He was rosy-cheeked from the ride over. 'Have the girls left yet?'

Tate shook his head. 'I don't think Mallory realizes how serious all this is. He sits comfortably behind his hired guns and thinks he's safe as a turkey in

46

a wire pen. But things are getting nasty down at the meeting hall.'

Jock sighed. His dark hair and deep blue eyes made him look a lot like his uncle, Certainty Sumner. But he was thin, and didn't have his full growth yet. 'I talked to Nell yesterday. She's scared, Uriah. She says the NPM men aren't afraid of the hired guns at the saloons, and that's bad.'

'Some of them are past asking for the girls to leave,' Tate said. 'They want the law to be enforced, and the saloons closed. They harangue me about that, and say I have to do my duty. But if I tried to close the saloons, I'd be dead by morning. Even L.C. Hartman in Dodge City hasn't tried to go that far.'

Jock looked over at him. 'No offense, Uriah. But you can't stand up against men like R.C. Wilson. And Webster is useless.'

'You don't have to tell me that, Jock. But I'll soon have to do something. I'm the law here in Sulphur Creek. Until the day I take this badge off.'

'Wyatt Earp rode in at Dodge and quieted things down,' Jock said. 'Too bad he didn't stop by here. I wish my uncle Wesley was alive. He'd make those self-satisfied gun-toters at the Prairie Schooner back off. Or my friend O'Brien.'

Tate regarded him curiously. 'O'Brien? That buffalo hunter whom your uncle partnered up with for a while?'

'Yeah, you met him when he visited me last year. He told me all about Wesley. We had a good time when he was here.'

'I met him, all right. Never saw such a tight-lipped man. Got a reputation for being unsociable.'

'He also has another reputation. Uncle Wesley told me the last time I saw him. He said O'Brien got in a fight once in a saloon in Tulsa, when a drifter insulted him. O'Brien was unarmed, but that didn't stop the drifter. As O'Brien came at him, he fired off three shots, and two hit O'Brien. But he came on through that hail of lead and beat the drifter to death with his bare hands.'

Tate shook his head slowly. 'That sounds like horse pucky.'

'Uncle Wesley said he heard it from a good source. He also told me that O'Brien can go two weeks on a can of beans and a bag of chicory, ride without sleep for most of that time, and hit a buffalo at a quarter-mile with the sun in his eyes.'

Tate let a slow smile cross his aging features. 'All right, all right. But your friend O'Brien is kind of like a drifter, Jock. No roots, no permanent ties. And he's in Colorado, you told me, in a different world. Get your head off of that, boy. You may never see that man again.' He paused. 'Jock, I heard something yesterday that involves you.'

Jock frowned. 'What is it, Uriah?'

'A cowpoke that was drinking at the Prairie Schooner heard Rabbit Purcell talking with the Mexican that Mallory hired.'

Jock nodded soberly.

'Purcell was talking about you, Jock. You must've really got under his skin that night at the saloon. You're in his craw.' He hesitated again. 'He says he's coming after you, Jock. And I think he's serious.'

Jock looked past Tate to the opposite wall, then met his gaze again. 'That pink-eye don't scare me.'

Tate sighed. 'That's not the reaction I wanted, Jock. This Purcell is dangerous, everybody knows it. He's got something wrong in his head. I told him what I'd heard, and he denied it. I can't arrest him, he ain't done nothing.'

'I told you I should be carrying,' Jock said. 'I let you talk me out of it.'

'You're fifteen years old, damn it!' Tate said irritably. Then his face softened. 'I been thinking it over. I got a Dardick 1500 .38 put away somewhere I can give you.'

Jock's eyes widened. 'That's great, Uriah!'

Tate sighed heavily.

'I can shoot,' Jock said excitedly. 'One

of the cowhands at the ranch has been letting me practice.'

'There's shooting and shooting,' Tate said quietly. 'You wouldn't be as good against Purcell as me, and that ain't good. I'd send you out of town if there was some place for you to go. Till this all cools down. Maybe you better stick out at the ranch more for a while.'

Jock averted his blue eyes. 'I meant to tell you. I quit out there.'

'What? When?'

'Just today. I hate the work, Uriah. I'm sorry. I was kind of hoping you'd deputize me.'

Tate frowned heavily. 'Do what?'

'Not to really make arrests or anything like that. Maybe clean up around the jail. Make evening rounds with you.'

'Sometimes, boy, you don't seem to have the sense you was born with,' Tate exclaimed hotly. 'I pulled strings to get you that job, damn it!'

Jock was about to respond to that dressing-down when a loud knocking

51

came at the cabin door. 'I reckon we'll discuss this later,' Tate said ruefully. Then he rose and went to answer the door. When he opened it, two drifters stood there.

'What is it, boys?' He assessed their tough looks.

'Is that Sulphur Creek up the trail there?' the taller one said.

Tate nodded. 'That's right.'

'Oh, good. We been riding all day. Is there any chance of a cup of coffee before we ride on in? We ain't got lodgings yet.'

Tate hesitated, then nodded. 'I can spare a cup. Why don't you step inside?'

They came on into the cabin, and Jock rose from the table. They looked over at him soberly. The fellow with the tall, thin man was thick-chested with several days' growth of beard and a milked-over left eye.

'Jock, fetch these two a cup of coffee,' Tate said. 'I'd ask you to sit, boys, but we're getting ready to bed down pretty soon here.'

The tall one nodded, and Jock delivered two cups of coffee to them. He decided he didn't like their looks much. 'You're heading into Sulphur Creek?' he said.

'That's right,' the brawny one answered. 'We heard the Prairie Schooner is hiring men with guns. Is that right?'

Jock and Tate exchanged a look. 'Yes, that's right,' Tate replied. 'But you boys are a mite late. Luke Mallory already hired everybody he'll be needing. I think it's the same at the Lost Dogie.'

The tall man glanced over at a vest hanging on a chair, with Tate's badge still on it. 'Oh, really. Would you by any chance be the law in this rat-hole of a town?'

'What the hell,' Jock muttered.

Tate regarded them somberly. 'I'm the law in Sulphur Creek,' he said. 'But it ain't no rat-hole, boys.'

'Then you probably wouldn't want any more guns at the Prairie Schooner,' the tall man went on with a grin.

Jock was worried. They both wore big

guns over their coats, and Tate had disarmed himself on his arrival home. The two were finished with the coffee now, and Jock took the cups and deposited them on a dry sink near double bunks toward the rear. He glanced at the lower bunk and spotted an eight-gauge shotgun lying there where Tate had just finished cleaning and reloading it when Jock arrived. Tate always kept the gun ready for use. The gun was partially hidden by a blanket.

'What I want don't always cut no grease in the saloons,' Tate was saying. 'Now if you boys got your fill of coffee, we got things to do here.'

The tall one came and put his foot up on a chair beside the table. 'You know what? I seen a lot of lawmen in my day, but you don't look like none I ever saw. What do you think, Ned?'

Ned looked Tate over arrogantly. 'I think this man's been posing as a marshal, hiding behind that badge over there. I bet this Mallory fellow would probably give us a big bonus if we put an end to this fakery tonight. We hear you're an enemy of the saloons here. We could give them a nice little present.'

'I'm going to have to ask you both to leave now,' Tate said, dry-mouthed. 'Before you break any laws here.'

'Actually we're looking for a place to bed down, and this little cabin might just fill the bill. Kill two birds with one stone, so to speak. What do you think, Ned?'

'I say we quit talking about it,' Ned said gutturally.

Jock took a step carefully backwards, without their noticing, and he was closer now to the shotgun. The brawny man named Ned casually drew the heavy revolver at his side. 'This will make us heroes to the saloon people. I'll do it.'

'You two will be hunted across several states,' Tate said tightly. 'The governor will send troops after you.'

'We're taking you two out back,' the tall man said, and he also drew his weapon. 'You got a shovel in here somewhere?'

'You pond scum!' Tate said loudly. 'We're not going anywhere!'

'You, kid!' the husky one said to Jock. 'Get on over here and tell this fool he better follow orders. We just want to talk to him out there.'

'OK,' Jock said. 'Just don't shoot him.'

Both guns went back on Tate for a moment. Jock reached unobtrusively to the bunk, grabbed the shotgun, and aimed it at the husky fellow, who was closer. He saw the movement and turned his gun back on Jock in a jerking motion, but it was too late. The shotgun roared out in the room and the husky man was slammed against the far wall, eyes bulging, his revolver firing into the floor. Tate had pulled his own revolver from its holster on a chair. The tall man now swung his revolver back toward Jock, who had been knocked against the bunks by the shotgun's recoil. Tate fired wildly, in a panic, hit an oil lamp in a corner, and then the tall man in the side, under his arm.

The tall drifter was slammed against the door not far from where his companion was now sliding to the floor, a bloody mess. When the tall man hit the door his gun was jarred loose from his grasp and clattered to his feet. He stared at Tate for a moment in shock and disbelief, then joined his partner on the wood-plank floor.

Jock was red-faced and breathless, and now aimed the double-barreled shotgun at the downed tall man to fire again.

'No, Jock!' Tate yelled across the room. 'It's over, boy! It's over.'

Jock set the shotgun down on the bunk, then collapsed against it again. Tate walked over to him, and saw that he was trembling all over. 'Take it easy, son. You did good.'

Jock looked over at the husky drifter. 'Did I kill him?'

Tate nodded. 'You did.'

'My God. I killed a man.'

'You had no choice, Jock. We had no choice. They was going to kill us.'

Jock walked weakly over to the two deceased gunmen, and stared down at them. He had never killed anything bigger than a red fox. He tried to assess how he felt. Tate came over and joined him. He didn't want to admit it to Jock at that moment, but it was the first time he had killed a man, too.

'They was going to take us out back and make us dig our own graves,' he said tiredly. 'That's the kind of weasel this town is attracting now.'

'I don't feel anything,' Jock said. He had stopped shaking. 'Shouldn't I feel something after killing someone?'

'Some men been known to throw up after the first one,' Tate said, feeling a little queazy himself. 'But I guess you got some of your uncle in you, son. You saved our skins with that eight-gauge.'

'I should feel bad about it. But I don't.'

'Feel glad to be alive,' Tate told him.

'I guess I do.'

Tate nodded. 'I reckon you are ready to strap on that Dardick. Just don't let it make you think you're something you're not, Jock. You're a green kid, no matter what just happened here. You understand?'

Jock nodded. 'I know, Uriah.'

'Come on then. We got to get these stiffs loaded on to their mounts. I want to go show them to Luke Mallory.'

3

O'Brien was already on his way south. He had cleaned out everything that belonged to him at the mountain cabin, and had taken his pelts to Fort Collins and sold them to a dealer there whom he had dealt with previously. He had obtained a good price for them. He sold the pack animal to the same dealer, because he didn't anticipate doing much trapping on the trail south.

The days were warmer now, and there were just small patches of snow in low-lying shaded areas. In a broad valley that he passed through the aspen trees had already started producing small green buds.

He had definitely resolved to stop at Sulphur Creek to meet with Jock Sumner, and although he looked forward to seeing the bounty hunter's nephew again, he wasn't anticipating with any pleasure the inevitable inter-play with the local citizenry that he always tolerated with barely hidden impatience. He disliked towns and town living, and all they stood for, always prefering the open plains and the wild country.

It was a several-days' ride into southern Kansas, and that gave O'Brien some nights on the trail. On the first night he fried up one of the bear steaks he had cut off after the grizzly attack, and had a few corn dodgers dipped in bear-fat grease. Partway through that night a heavy rain swept in from the west, and forced him up to protect his provisions and equipment. The Appaloosa gave him no trouble.

The second day out, though, was sunny and fairly warm. Now he was on his way into Kansas, and as he rode he noticed that some ranches had been replaced by small farms where corn and wheat were being grown. When he rode past a couple of the big ranches, he would see a tight little herd of cattle grazing in a box canyon, or along some small stream.

In the afternoon he found himself out in open country and recalled how thick it used to be with buffalo. In those days he had spent much of his time crawling up on a herd on his belly, 'like a goddam snake', getting in close with the Sharps rifle. He missed those days. Nobody could know what it was like except another buffalo hunter.

In late afternoon he got a surprise. In open range, only a few miles from a big ranch, he crested a low rise of ground and there they were. A herd of shaggies.

It was a very small herd, only a couple dozen animals or so, and several of them were just calves, which O'Brien never shot. But the vista gave him a warm feeling inside, a nostalgia that was very emotional. They hadn't seen him. They were quietly chewing their cuds in a gentle westerly breeze and sunning themselves in the mild warmth of a rock outcropping.

There were two big bulls, and one

had a robe-quality coat. O'Brien couldn't afford to pass them up. It was a fortuitous moment that had to be seized. He dismounted from the stallion, and went to the saddle scabbard that held the big Sharps rifle and its tripod. The stallion seemed nervous and, as he slid the heavy gun from its moorings, he heard a rumble of thunder off to the west. He looked in that direction and saw that thick, dark clouds had gathered and were moving in fast.

'Damn!' he swore softly.

He picketed the horse to a stake from his saddle wallet and headed on over the rise of ground with the big gun. Another clap of thunder sounded, closer, with lightning flashes. He had to hurry. The herd looked a little restless, but were still standing quietly. The big bull with the beautiful coat turned and looked toward the approaching storm.

O'Brien set up the tripod carefully. They hadn't seen him yet. He grabbed the long gun and was raising it up to the tripod when a bright bolt of lightning came crashing down almost on top of the herd. It split a nearby cottonwood tree wide open, leaving a scarred, smoking ruin.

The blast was followed by a clap of thunder that roared in O'Brien's ears. Suddenly the buffalo herd was on the move, stampeding away from O'Brien just as he was securing the rifle to the tripod. By the time he had knelt down beside the weapon the shaggies were disappearing behind a low out-cropping of boulders over 500 yards away.

'Sonofabitch!' he growled out, watching the herd disappear from sight. He tore his hat off and threw it on to the ground beside him, then just sat there bare-headed as rain began pelting him.

That was the way it was with buff hunting; it always had been. There were always unpredictable factors to wreck the hunt. You could track and stalk a herd for days and then have it all go sour on you. If these animals had stampeded toward him instead of away, they might have killed him under their hoofs. He had finished his hunt one time about three years ago, when a prairie fire swept over him and his kills. He had gutted a big bull just before the fire arrived, crawled into its rib cage, and let the fire roar on over him. The buffalo had had all its fur burned away, and some of its meat cooked to a turn, but O'Brien had survived the fire, singed and choking.

'This might've been my last chance ever, the way things are going,' he said aloud, grabbing his discarded Stetson to ward off a light rain. Now that the herd was gone, he could see some blue patches of sky overhead.

He looked up at the clearing sky. 'Wouldn't you know it?' he added.

The interlude wasn't a complete loss, though. Before he could return the rifle to its scabbard a big, hungry-looking wolf appeared over at the tree line, and was eyeing the stallion. O'Brien took it down with one clean shot before it could cause him or his mount any trouble.

That night he made camp on the bank of a small river, and finished off the last of the bear steaks. There was good grazing for the Appaloosa, and the night was clear and cool for sleeping.

Tomorrow he would be in Sulphur Creek.

* * *

That same evening, Luke Mallory and Hank Logan, the saloon-keepers of Sulphur Creek, met at the Lost Dogie saloon with their hired gunmen.

Uriah Tate had brought the two dead drifters to the doorstep of the Prairie Schooner and accused Mallory of creating a lawless atmosphere in the area that allowed men like the dead gunmen to think they could get away with murder. Mallory denied any responsibility for the two men, and shouted at Tate that he had become a bleeding-heart reformer himself. Mallory declared him an enemy and unfit to wear his badge.

66

Now the two saloon-owners had gotten together to discuss the threat of the reform group, and what to do about it and Uriah Tate.

They had gathered in the back room of the Lost Dogie. Mallory, Logan, Wilson and Logan's only hired gun Maynard McComb all sat at a big round card table in the center of the room. Rabbit Purcell sat on a stool in a corner near the door, and Pedro Rueda, Mallory's third gunman, leaned against a nearby wall, smoking a cigarillo.

'That damned Avery Hawkins went to the governor to demand saloon closures, and to enforce the dry laws,' Logan was saying. 'I told you he was trouble.'

Mallory grunted. 'The governor drinks like the rest of us,' he said. 'He was against the dry law. Everybody knows that. If he closed saloons here, he'd have to close them all over the state. Can you imagine how they'd take that over in Dodge?'

'The problem is,' R.C. Nilson spoke

up, 'he don't want this kind of spotlight on him. His political enemies can use that against him.'

Both Mallory and Logan glanced over at him. Mallory knew that Wilson was a cut above men like Purcell. But he didn't want him to be too smart. Men like him had been known to take over whole towns.

Mallory nodded. 'That's right, Wilson. That's why we have to do something about Hawkins and his little crew. They have that hot-head St Clair over there now. I don't think he'd really have the guts to try to set fire to a saloon like he's been yelling about. But he's trouble.'

'Leave him to me,' Wilson volunteered with a grin.

Logan's man McComb looked over at Wilson somberly. He was a husky redhead with a pockmarked lower face and a scar along his windpipe that made him speak in a grating half-whisper. He was an old drinking crony of Hank Logan. 'We ain't ready for no shooting, Wilson.'

Wilson regarded him diffidently. 'Maybe it's just you that ain't ready.'

McComb's face quickly clouded over, and Mallory intervened. 'All right, boys. Nobody's shooting anybody. We're just talking here.'

'I think Wilson is right,' Purcell said from his stool. The albino was paring his nails with a penknife and hadn't bothered to look up when he spoke. Rueda, against the wall, grinned through his black mustache.

'Do your hired guns dictate policy over there at the Schooner?' McComb persisted heatedly.

'It's all right, Maynard,' Logan said easily. 'That's why we're here. To get everybody's opinions out into the open. Do we have any influence with the governor, Luke?'

'Maybe a little,' Mallory replied, shooting a look at Purcell. 'We could draft a letter. Get a lot of signatures on it. He might be impressed.'

'By that time, they might've burnt your building down,' Wilson said.

'Throw a scare into the *cobardes*,' Rueda called out past his diminutive cigar. 'Go to their meetings. All of us.'

Mallory regarded him thoughtfully. 'Actually, that's not a bad idea.'

Logan nodded agreement. 'We could do that. Everybody go in armed. Make a show of force.'

Rueda grinned broadly. People didn't usually pay much attention to him.

'It's a halfway measure,' Wilson offered.

'You know, I'm getting tired of hearing from you, Wilson,' Maynard McComb said to him soberly.

Wilson's dark eyes flashed fire at him. 'Maybe you ought to try to shut me up.'

'Damn it, you two!' Mallory exclaimed loudly. 'We're all on the same side here! Save this for the reformers!'

McComb sighed. 'My fault, Luke. Forget I said anything.'

'That's better,' Logan said. 'Look, when does the NPM meet again?'

'They're scheduled for Thursday. A

couple days from now, at seven,' Wilson said.

They all looked over at him. Mallory was the unofficial leader of their group but everybody there knew that Wilson could challenge that situation at any moment. His gun commanded that kind of respect.

'Good,' Mallory said without inflection. 'That's good, Wilson. Any objections to showing up at the meeting hall Thursday, boys?'

Nobody spoke. 'Then that's settled,' Mallory concluded.

'Now. What about Uriah Tate?' Logan said. He was older than the rest of them. He was almost bald, and paunchy. He wore green sleeve garters and could quote world news.

'We've put up with that snake long enough,' Rabbit Purcell chimed in again. He looked like a ghost sitting there on the stool, with his deathly-pale skin, his pink, translucent irises, and his shaggy white hair protruding from all sides of his dark hat. 'I say, run him out

71

of town on a rail. Or better yet, catch him in a dark alley some night. Preferably with that kid that follows him around. Then it's two for the price of one.' He gave a scary grin.

Wilson returned the grin, liking the discomfort that Purcell always caused the rest of them.

'You're suggesting we murder the city marshal?' Logan said in irritation.

Purcell shrugged.

'Mayor Provost would never stand for anything like that,' Mallory said acidly to his henchman. 'Like I said before, we don't want interference from the governor.' Mallory now hated Tate, and would celebrate his demise by gunfire. But he didn't want to be the one who issued his death warrant. 'And if you decide to take any action against that Sumner kid, it better not come back on me.'

Purcell grinned again. 'That's private business, Mallory. Don't sweat it.'

Logan and McComb had no idea what they were talking about. Logan brought the discussion back to Tate. 'The marshal has been pretty quiet lately, anyway. Has he asked again about the girls?'

Mallory shook his head. 'No, but I got a feeling he'll be back. He's had a wild hair up his backside ever since those drifters tried to kill him.'

'Too bad they didn't,' Wilson said. 'We could start making this town ours.'

Mallory allowed his face to assume a long, sober look. Logan cleared his throat. 'Well, one last thing. Luke and me been talking. We ought to show the town that we're united. Do what they did in Dodge City. Call ourselves the Sulphur Creek Peace Commission. A kind of arm of the law, in our own saloons. Provost will put his stamp of approval on it, with a twist of his arm.'

'That's right,' Mallory said. 'It will give us a legitimacy in the eyes of the locals. The ranchers are already behind us.'

Wilson grunted in his throat.

'Sounds smart,' McComb said.

'Any objections?' Mallory asked, looking at Wilson.

'Then I'll see the mayor tomorrow,' Logan concluded.

* * *

The next morning, just before noon, Uriah Tate arrived at the Prairie Schooner with his deputy Webster.

Jock Sumner was living with Tate now and had been hired to do odd jobs around the jail. He had been left there to take care of the office while Tate and his only deputy were gone to the saloon, where Tate planned to arrest Big Betty and Nita Ruiz, the saloon girls who had refused to leave Mallory's employ. If things went well here, Tate would do the same thing at the Lost Dogie, and arrest the mayor's favorite, Rose Nicely. Jock had advised Tate to wait till things cooled off, but Tate was in no mood for waiting.

When Tate and Webster arrived there was already a small crowd of drinkers present, and all eyes turned on them as they came through the swinging doors. Not far from the doors, Wilson and Purcell sat eating boiled eggs and swigging beer. They both stopped eating when they spotted the two lawmen.

'Well, look at this,' Wilson purred out.

Luke Mallory was talking with a customer at the rear of the room, and Big Betty stood at the long bar. Nita, a dark-haired Latina, was behind the bar with the heavy-set bartender. Everything in the place came to a halt as Mallory walked toward Tate and Webster.

'Well, Marshal. I see you can't take a hint. I thought I'd made it clear you're not welcome in the Schooner. But now that you're here, I can sell you a bottle to go.'

'I'm not here to buy liquor,' Tate told him gruffly.

'Yeah, he's not here to buy liquor,' Webster echoed him. He was a man with vacant-looking eyes, bad teeth, and sloppy clothes. He wore an old Webley-Pryce .476 revolver low on his hip, but was useless with it.

'I've come for Betty,' Tate said firmly. He had noticed Wilson and Purcell at their table, and was feeling tension. 'And Nita.'

Mallory sighed. 'I thought we went through this, Tate. We haven't decided on that yet. These girls are valuable to the saloon.'

'I know their worth to you,' Tate replied. 'But that don't make no difference now. I'm doing you a favor, Luke. Keeping them reform people off your back.'

'Let me worry about the reform people,' Mallory said. 'And I know that Hawkins saw the governor. That means nothing.'

Tate sighed heavily. 'Webster, take Betty and Nita outside. Use cuffs if you have to. I'm through talking about this.'

Webster walked over to Betty, who shied away from him. 'I'm not going anywhere with you, you little flea-brain,' she cried.

Webster looked over at Tate.

'Sounds like she doesn't want to go.' Mallory smiled.

'Cuff her,' Tate barked out.

'I wouldn't do that.' Mallory quickly intervened. He cast a glance toward his gunmen who had both risen from their table, their hands near their weapons. Tate's face crimsoned.

'Are you threatening an officer of the law?' he grated out.

'Not at all. I'm just saying my girls are staying right here, Tate. I don't recognize your authority here in the Schooner.'

'What the hell do you mean?' Tate spat out.

'Didn't you hear? We formed a Peace Commission. You know, as a kind of supplement to your authority. The mayor approved it early this morning. The commission's authority governs in these saloons, Marshal. And the commission says the girls stay.'

Over at the bar Big Betty giggled.

'That's the truth of it, Marshal,' Wilson said from the table. 'Now why don't you get to hell out of here? You're disturbing the peace!'

'You can't talk to the marshal that way!' Webster protested from the bar.

'Are you and your thugs trying to set yourselves up as the law in Sulphur Creek?' Tate said, ignoring Wilson. 'Is that what's going on here, you bastard? I'm the elected marshal in this town, by Jesus, and I intend to uphold the law here!'

'Tate is the law here!' Webster said loudly.

'You're only one part of it now, Tate,' Mallory said. 'The Peace Commission is the other part. And we vote to keep the girls on.'

Tate almost drew his Colt, but quickly thought better of it. He was being forced to back down again, and he was embarrassed and angry.

'This is obstruction of justice, by God. Your commission don't have no standing in Sulphur Creek.'

'Oh?' Mallory smiled irritatingly. 'Maybe you better talk to our mayor about that.'

'I will!' Tate almost shouted. 'This town ain't going to be took over by a gang of hoodlums!'

Wilson and Purcell were still standing. 'Who are you calling a hoodlum, Marshal?' Wilson said from across the room.

'Yeah,' Purcell added. 'You casting slurs on these nice folks in here?'

'You know who I'm talking about,' Tate replied, more subdued now. He turned back to Mallory. 'This ain't the last of this, Mallory.'

Mallory's smile widened. 'I think it is, Marshal.'

'Come on, Webster. Let's go get us some fresh air outside. This place has got a stink to it that makes a man sick.'

'Don't you mean yellow?' Rabbit Purcell grinned.

Wilson and several drinking patrons laughed quietly.

'Let me arrest him!' Webster yelled.

Purcell laughed again.

Tate hurled a look of hatred at him, but decided not to reply. He refused to be goaded into a shoot-out that would leave the town without any law. He nodded toward the door, and Webster reluctantly preceded him through it. When they got out onto the street, Tate grabbed a pair of handcuffs from his belt and threw them into the dirt at his feet. Then he strode off toward the jail without looking back.

Webster watched him go for a long moment, then picked up the cuffs and followed his boss on down the street.

* * *

It was only just over two hours later that O'Brien rode into Sulphur Creek on his tired Appaloosa. The town looked the same as it had when he had visited Jock Sumner just over a year ago, except that now there were two churches and a school, and the town was encircled by small farms where sharecroppers were raising pigs, chickens and milk cows. Everything was changing, and it made him uncomfortable. Civilization was coming to the West. He could understand the hostility of the ranchers and saloon people toward the newcomers. They sensed, like the Lakota and Pawnee before them, that a wild way of life was being eroded, and that once gone, it would never return.

When O'Brien had been here a year ago, Jock had been living with a relative now deceased, and O'Brien had no idea which ranch Jock had been working for, so when he arrived at the local hostelry at the south end of town he decided to inquire there.

He gave the Appaloosa over and got it unsaddled before he spoke much to the hostler.

'He might be here a few days,' he told the other fellow. 'Treat him like he belongs to the governor. If you don't, I'll know it.'

The dumpy, round-faced hostler looked the big hunter over. O'Brien had shed a sheepskin jacket now, in view of the warmer weather, and wore only his rawhides. The shirt was belted at the waist with a wide ammo belt, but the ammunition was for his Winchester. As usual, he wore no sidearm.

'Anything you say, mister. I don't think I caught your name.'

'I didn't give it,' O'Brien said gruffly. 'You'll know me when I come back. Just see that that animal eats better than you do.'

The hostler hesitated. 'Certainly.' He squinted down. 'Say, would you be that buffalo hunter they call O'Brien?'

O'Brien had turned to his mount, but now he turned back, dropping a brittle look on the hostler. Already it had started. He hated towns.

'I thought you tended horses. You got a second job at the damn local newspaper?'

The hostler stepped back without knowing he had done it. 'No offense,

82

mister. I just heard some stories, that's all. Just forget I asked.'

'I already did. You ever hear of a kid named Jock Sumner?'

'Oh, sure. He's working for Marshal Tate.'

O'Brien frowned. 'Are you sure?'

'Yes, I think he's even living with him now. Out at Tate's cabin. But you'd probably find him down at the jail. He works there, helping out. A good kid. But if you want to talk with him, maybe you better not wait.'

'What does that mean?'

'I hear one of Luke Mallory's men, an albino called Purcell, is out gunning for the kid.'

O'Brien's face clouded over. 'Is that right?' His expression became pensive. That had been the ill-hidden feeling in Jock's last letter to him.

'The kid is good as dead. Purcell is a real killer.'

O'Brien focused on him. 'I don't think I like you, hostler.'

The other man swallowed hard.

'Sorry. It's what everybody is saying. I might be wrong.'

O'Brien pointed a thick finger into his face. 'If that Appaloosa don't look like a show horse when I get back here, I'm going to skin you and sell your mangy hide to the Indians.'

The hostler tried a nervous grin. 'You don't have to worry about that none. I'll treat him like Queen Victoria herself owned him!'

O'Brien grunted and left the place on foot. As he walked toward the marshal's office he recalled from his previous visit that the Luke Mallory the hostler had refered to owned one of the saloons in town; he surmised that the man called Purcell must have been hired to put the fear of God into the recently arrived reformers.

The jail that housed Tate's office was a rather small clapboard building with one window, at the front beside the entrance. O'Brien pushed through the door and let his eyes adjust to the lack of direct sunlight, his riding spurs clicking metallically in the silence inside. The interior was white-washed and had a clean, antiseptic look. An old weathered desk stood against a wall to his right, and a potbelly stove was on the left, with the fire guttered out. On the wall above the stove was a bulletin board with several Wanted dodgers affixed to it, a couple looking ancient. There was a smell of wood ash from the stove. A hall led to the rear, where O'Brien could glimpse a cellblock.

'Anybody here?' he called out in his deep voice.

In a moment, Uriah Tate appeared in the short corridor, coming toward him. As he came into the room he looked O'Brien over. 'I'll be damned! It's Jock's friend O'Brien, ain't it?'

'The same,' O'Brien told him. Tate extended his hand, and O'Brien took it. Tate was sorry he had made the effort, squinting in pain under the iron grip. 'Good to see you again.'

O'Brien released Tate's hand. Tate rubbed it and grinned. 'I remember that from last year.'

O'Brien didn't understand at first. 'Oh. Sorry. That's the hand I cut the pelts off with.' He gave a half-grin. 'How's everything in Sulphur Creek?'

Tate made a sour face. 'I could write you a book. Say, Jock is out back. Did he know you're coming?'

O'Brien shook his head. 'I ain't much at letter-writing.'

Tate turned to the corridor. 'Jock! You got a visitor!'

Jock came out of a cell where he was changing some bedding, and squinted down the hallway. Then his face changed.

'O'Brien?'

O'Brien smiled at him. 'Hi, kid,' he greeted the youth, with a genuine warmth in his voice that was rare for him.

Jock hurried to them with a wide, happy grin on his handsome young face. When he reached O'Brien, he surprised the hunter by throwing his arms around him.

'O'Brien! Damn!'

O'Brien was embarrassed. Nobody ever thought of him as embraceable, not even the rare saloon girl he had coupled with on occasion.

'Hey, hey. Take it easy there, kid. I'm not your long-lost aunt. You'll get the stink of beaver pelts on you.'

Jock stepped back and looked O'Brien over. 'You're exactly like I remembered. I dreamt you'd show up here, you know.'

O'Brien was shaking his head and grinning. 'I'm on my way south. I got your note and decided to stop here a couple of days. Nice to see you again, Jock. You're looking all growed up now. And I see you're carrying iron.'

'I told him he could,' Tate put in. 'We had a little scare out at my cabin.'

'A couple of drifters,' Jock said. 'We took care of them.'

'Jock had to kill one of them,' Tate said soberly.

O'Brien looked back at Jock and studied his youthful face. 'I guess you are a man now.' He was sorry to hear it.

Killing a man makes you grow up in a minute, he knew. It takes your innocence away. 'You're the spitting image, you know. Of your uncle.'

'I'm glad to hear that,' Jock said, still grinning widely. 'Are you going to take me out hunting again, O'Brien?'

O'Brien nodded. 'We might go out after some quail and rabbit before I leave. After the Appaloosa gets rested up.'

'Uncle Wesley said you're the best hunter since Daniel Boone,' Jock said.

'Your uncle's judgment was clouded a little by our closeness.' O'Brien smiled at him. 'But he was a Webster with guns. Nobody ever wanted to face him down. The marshal here can tell you.'

'Why don't you wear a sidearm, O'Brien?' Jock had never thought to ask that question before.

O'Brien's square face went sober. 'Never had no need for one, kid. All they do is invite trouble.'

Jock glanced down at the Dardick

revolver on his hip.

'Jock's situation is different,' Tate interjected. 'He's had some trouble here in town.'

O'Brien looked over at Tate, and realized the marshal would offer little more protection for Jock than the gun on Jock's hip. 'I heard,' he said.

Jock and Tate exchanged a quick glance. 'It's really nothing,' Jock said. 'Just some blow-hard over at the Prairie Schooner.'

O'Brien went over and sat on the corner of Tate's old desk. 'I understand the reformers have descended on you, Marshal. Causing you all kinds of trouble.'

Tate nodded. 'This is a hard bunch, O'Brien. They want action that I can't give them. And the saloon owners have hired guns to answer the threat. It's an explosive situation, and I ain't equipped to handle it. I'm not that good with a gun, and my deputy used to clean stables for a living.'

O'Brien let out a long breath. He

hadn't wanted to walk into the middle of someone else's troubles while he was here. 'Why don't you run the reformers out of town?' he said. 'Everybody knows these dry laws in Kansas are headed for repeal eventually.'

Tate shook his head. 'It's past that. They're dug in. And these gunmen are sitting in those saloons with itchy trigger-fingers. Just hoping they can draw down on somebody.' He told O'Brien about the new Peace Commission. 'I talked to the mayor. I told him that was vigilantism. But he says I need that kind of help here in town, and that it worked in Dodge. He's always been in the back pocket of the saloon owners.'

'Sounds like you're in a hard place,' O'Brien said.

'Oh, we'll muddle through it some-how,' Tate offered.

'If you don't get yourself killed,' Jock said.

O'Brien studied the boy's solemn face. It was clear that he had become very close to Tate, and was concerned about his survival.

'Don't worry your head about me, Jock,' Tate told him. 'I been through tough times before.'

O'Brien got off the desk. 'I see there's a little hotel down the street there, not far from the Prairie Schooner. You think they could find me a bed here for a couple nights?'

Tate squinted his eyes down. 'I'd put you up myself, but I got no room. Hey. You could sleep right here at the jail if you don't mind a hard, skinny mattress in one of the cells. We got nobody back there right now.'

O'Brien looked toward the rear, and a half-grin crossed his trail-dusty features. 'That would suit me right down to the ground.'

'That's great!' Jock exclaimed. 'I'll see you all the time then!'

Tate smiled at the boy's enthusiasm. 'It's settled then. Jock, go get that end cell ready.'

'Done!' Jock grinned. Then he left

the room, and O'Brien was alone with Tate.

'Now,' he said quietly. 'What's this about some piece of swamp slime called Purcell threatening this boy?' He spoke in a low, flat voice.

Tate turned quickly to him, and saw the changed look on the hunter's face, a look that he had never seen there before. He sighed heavily. 'Yes. Rabbit Purcell. An albino pale as a linen napkin. And a stone killer.'

'He said he's coming after Jock?'

'That's the word. And I think we have to take him seriously. That's the real reason I let Jock start wearing a gun, and gave him a job here at the jail, where I can keep an eye on him. Of course, he's with me at night. But I'm secretly worried over it. I can't watch him every minute. I try not to talk much about it with him.'

'What caused all the ruckus?'

'Oh, Jock went into the Schooner one night to get our WCTU woman out of there and Purcell got involved. Jock insulted Purcell, and Purcell knocked him down. I come in then and got Jock out of there. But Purcell went crazy about the insult, and vowed to find Jock and kill him.'

O'Brien was standing there absorbing all of that when Jock bustled back into the room, looking very pleased with himself. 'I got it all ready for you, O'Brien.' He smiled happily. 'You're our jailhouse guest now.'

O'Brien returned the smile. It was good to see the boy again. 'I'll get my gear from the hostelry later. But for now, why don't we all walk down to the hotel and put some chow down?'

Tate nodded. It gave him a new, unexpected sense of security to have the buffalo hunter here in town.

'I was about to suggest the same thing myself,' he said.

4

Uriah Tate drove O'Brien, Jock and himself out to his cabin in the early evening in an old buckboard he kept in back of the jail, and O'Brien had a nice quiet talk with Jock. There were few persons O'Brien would sit and 'jaw' with more than five miutes, but young Jock was one of them. For O'Brien, it was almost like talking with Jock's uncle.

In the meantime the Sulphur Creek chapter of the National Prohibition Movement had set their Thursday meeting forward to this night because they got wind of Luke Mallory's plan to attend their regularly scheduled meeting. The ploy didn't work, though, because the saloon crowd showed up partway through the meeting. Their chairman, Avery Hawkins, had been speaking to the small assemblage of members, their families, and a scattering of sympathetic town-folk at the time.

'We have to put pressure on the retailers, too,' Hawkins was telling the room at the meeting hall. 'I've already spoken to both store owners about their sales of retail liquor, but so far we've had no cooperation.' He and his two assistants were seated at a table on a raised stage, and Nell Douglas, the WCTU activist, sat with them. Hawkins was flanked by Ned Turner, a thin, slightly stooped fellow with transparent hair, and Will St Clair, the NPM hot-head, an owlish man with heavy brows and a handlebar mustache who rarely smiled. He had brazenly suggested, a few weeks ago, that the saloons should be burned down to make room for 'respectable businesses'.

'I'll talk to them,' St Clair volunteered. He thought Hawkins and Tanner employed too soft an approach.

Hawkins was about to reply to him when the saloon men came in. Luke

Mallory and Hank Logan came in first, followed by their four 'protectors'.

The newcomers fanned out along the back wall, without seeking seats. Everybody in the room stared at them.

Hawkins had a solemn look on his square face with its jutting jaw. 'Luke, you and Hank are always welcome at our meetings. But your hired guns aren't.'

There was a scattered murmur of agreement from those present.

Mallory smiled easily. 'First of all, Avery, these men are bouncers at our establishments. Hired to keep the peace. That's why we call ourselves the Peace Commission. You're in favor of peace here in the NPM, aren't you?'

'You know we are.' Hawkins glared at him.

'Well, then. And secondly, if we're welcome here, why did you change the meeting time so secretly?'

'Look around you,' Hawkins said. 'Does this look like a secret meeting?'

'Why don't you just get on with it?'

Logan suggested, standing beside Mallory.

'Yeah,' R.C. Wilson the gunfighter called out. 'We want to hear all your plans, Hawkins!'

St Clair's wife stood up and turned to the men at the rear. 'None of you is welcome here! You're the enemy! We don't have to share our plans with the enemy! I think I speak for everybody here when I say, leave and take your hired thugs with you!'

Another murmuring of approval came from the crowd.

'Maybe I'm wrong, but I thought this is a public meeting hall, folks. And we're citizens of Sulphur Creek, too.'

'And we don't have to have our women speak for us.' Wilson grinned.

Purcell and Rueda both uttered quiet laughs. McComb, standing beside Hank Logan, looked over at Wilson soberly.

'In our families, our women speak as freely as we do,' Hawkins said.

St Clair came around the table where they sat, putting on a bold front. 'And you don't intimidate us by bringing these trail bums in here!' he said loudly. 'So take them on back to your drinking palaces. They don't belong among decent people!'

Wilson started to respond to that insult, but Rabbit Purcell beat him to it. He stepped forward and into the aisle that led to the platform where St Clair stood, so there was no impediment between them.

'Who the hell are you calling a trail bum, you little piss-ant! Who says we ain't decent people?'

St Clair knew he had gone too far. He did a lot of swaggering and loud talking, but he was no gunman. The trouble was, he couldn't let Purcell make him look bad in front of all these people who believed in the cause.

He hesitated a long moment. 'You know what you are, Purcell. You don't need me to tell you.'

Purcell's pale face turned pink quickly. 'And I know what you are, yellow-belly! Defend yourself, you goddam worm!'

'Now, hold it, Purcell!' Hawkins shouted, rising from his seat.

But for St Clair there was no way out. After all the blustering he had done around town he couldn't let this hated lowlife humiliate him. Anyway, he thought, his cheeks flushed, this wasn't Wilson. He might just beat Purcell.

'What's the matter, yellow-belly?' Purcell said breathlessly. 'Afraid to show everybody you're just a blow-hard?'

St Clair's face had twisted up in anguish, and suddenly his hand went for the Tranter .38 on his hip. Hawkins saw the movement and yelled out again.

'Will! No!'

But the revolver was already on its way out of its holster. Purcell had seen the movement, too, and his .45 cleared leather a second sooner than the Tranter. It exploded loudly in the big room.

St Clair's gun roared out, too, making a double reverberation echo around the hall. At the same moment,

Purcell's hot lead struck him like a hammer in the chest, punching him back into the table where the members sat. His slug tore at Purcell's vest, but missed him and buried itself in the closed door behind him.

St Clair slid slowly on to his side in front of the table, lifeless, as gunsmoke filled nostrils and a heavy silence settled into the room. Then one lone woman screamed out shrilly from the crowd.

Now there was a general commotion from the assemblage, as Purcell, with an arrogant grin, holstered his weapon. Mallory and Logan exchanged a sober look, and Logan's man McComb stared hard at Purcell. 'Have you gone nuts?' he growled out.

Avery Hawkins had rushed around to the front of the table where St Clair lay, while Nell Douglas almost fainted. Hawkins bent over St Clair and felt for a pulse. Then he looked up at the crowd. 'He's dead,' he muttered in disbelief.

A loud gasping sounded from the crowd.

Hawkins rose, and pointed an accusing finger at Mallory. 'This is murder, Luke! And you're responsible!'

Mallory was shaking his head. 'Wilson, go on back to the saloon and take these with you.'

Wilson had been enjoying the whole thing. He shrugged and motioned to Purcell and the others.

'He drew down on me!' Purcell called out to Hawkins. 'Everybody here saw it!' Then he left with Wilson and Rueda. McComb turned to a stunned Logan. 'That's it,' he growled. 'Count me out of this.' Then he left, too.

Mallory turned back to face Hawkins and the others in the room. 'This was a very unfortunate turn of events. One which I deeply regret. But Purcell was right. He was insulted. And when he challenged St Clair, the fool drew on him. Purcell had to defend himself.'

The crowd had quieted down now.

Nell had come around to pray over St Clair's body, and the other NPM man, Ned Turner, had joined Hawkins beside Nell.

'This was cold-blooded murder, Mallory! St Clair was goaded into this by that killer, and you know it! Marshal Tate will hear about this!'

'Why, of course he will,' Mallory replied. 'I intend to report it myself. Purcell may want to file charges against St Clair and the NPM. I'll discuss it with him.'

'Charges against us!' Hawkins yelled, red-faced. 'You've gone too far, Mallory! Logan! This town will be up in arms against you now!'

Mallory smiled. 'We'll see,' he said pleasantly. 'And again, I'm very sorry for this tragic incident, which was entirely avoidable. Well, good evening, all.'

Logan nodded and tipped his hat to the room, then they were gone.

* * *

As Mallory had suspected, the town didn't rise up against the saloon owners and their hired guns. In fact, now a fear settled over Sulphur Creek such as the town had never experienced before. Cowboys still came into town to put down booze at the two saloons that night, but townsfolk stayed at home, deathly afraid of the Peace Commission guns, and especially of the out-of-control and unpredictable Rabbit Purcell. Everyone present at the meeting-hall incident had little doubt that if St Clair hadn't drawn on Purcell, Purcell would have shot him down, anyway.

It was still early evening when the meeting broke up and St Clair's body was taken to the local morgue. Avery Hawkins knew that Uriah Tate had gone home for the evening with Jock Sumner and a stranger, leaving the deputy Webster in charge at the jail, so Hawkins rode out to Tate's cabin as soon as he was finished at the morgue.

When he arrived at the cabin Tate, Jock and O'Brien were sitting around

Tate's table drinking coffee and listening to Tate tell about his dealings with Mallory and Logan. O'Brien's big, broad-shouldered frame dominated the room. Whenever he entered a place most folks present turned their attention warily on to him. He gave off an aura that made other men rest a hand close to their sidearms.

'Mallory and me got along pretty well till the reformers came in,' Tate was saying. 'But we're nose to nose now.'

'He's as bad as the men he hired,' Jock said. 'He knows better, and they don't.'

O'Brien looked over at Jock, and was surprised at the accuracy of the observation. He was bare-headed, and his wild, ucombed shock of dark hair gave him a very primitive look. 'Ordinary men can turn mean when they're pushed into a corner,' he said quietly.

Jock turned to look at his friend with a half-smile. It was great how much better he felt about it all, with O'Brien here. He was about to agree with O'Brien's remark when the knock came at the door. When Tate answered it, Hawkins stood there, out of breath.

'St Clair is dead!' he gasped.

Tate screwed his face up. 'What?'

'I'm telling you. Will is dead, and that sub-human Purcell killed him. Shot him down like a dog!' Sweat was standing on his forehead.

Tate let a long breath out slowly. 'Come on in, Avery.'

Avery entered the cabin, and took a chair Tate offered him. He looked very distraught. 'I'm telling you, Marshal. Something has to be done about this.'

Tate nodded and seated himself again at the table. 'Yes, of course. You know Jock, I think, Avery. This fellow beside him there is a friend, O'Brien.'

O'Brien nodded his head. This was the first time he had ever met a reformer. He couldn't help wondering why they felt the need to cause so much trouble. If they wanted a God-fearing, civilized place to live, there were plenty of them back East.

'Glad to meet you, O'Brien,' Hawkins managed, despite his upset. 'Excuse my manner tonight. This has been a bad evening.'

'Now, you say it was Purcell?' Tate asked him.

'It's always Purcell,' Hawkins said. 'Wilson is the deadliest with a gun. But Purcell is a crazy, hot-headed killer who can't wait to use that weapon of his. He terrifies women in the local stores. Insulting them in front of their menfolk. His looks alone would scare crows out of a cornfield. And now look what he's done.'

'Is this the same man who threatened Jock here?' O'Brien asked.

'The same,' Tate told him. 'You can see now why I let Jock start carrying.' He turned to Hawkins. 'Was St Clair armed?'

Hawkins sighed. 'Yes. But Purcell goaded him into drawing first. And he knew that would be suicide for St Clair.'

Tate blew his cheeks out. 'I see what you mean.'

'That bastard!' Jock spat out.

'The NPM will expect you to do something about this, Marshal. The citizens of Sulphur Creek will expect it!'

Tate sighed heavily. 'I know, Hawkins. I know.' He clapped a hand on to the other man's shoulder. 'Did you take care of the body?'

'It's already down at the morgue.'

'Good. I'll talk to a couple of your members tomorrow morning, to verify details. In the meantime, you go on home and let me handle it. And don't get no ideas of taking action on your own. You hear me?'

Hawkins nodded. 'I understand, Marshal. But something has to be done about this.'

'You just go on home now,' Tate told him.

A moment later Hawkins was gone, and the cabin was suddenly very quiet. After a moment Tate turned to O'Brien. 'Sorry to end the evening early,

O'Brien. But I guess it's about time to take you back to town.'

'You realize you have nothing to arrest Purcell on,' O'Brien said.

Tate met his gaze with a tired one. 'I know. Jock, you stay here. I'll be back before bedtime.'

'I'm going with you,' Jock said emotionally.

Tate looked over at Jock.

'Maybe that's the safest thing for him,' O'Brien suggested.

Tate hesitated. 'OK. Let's go.'

They all got aboard the buckboard wagon again, and drove into town. There was almost no talking among them on the way. When they arrived at the jail, Tate's deputy Webster was sitting with his feet up at Tate's desk. He jumped to his feet when the three of them entered. He had been on the verge of going to sleep. He looked disheveled in his wrinkled, worn-out clothing, his stringy hair uncombed.

'Marshal! I thought you was done for the night.' He glanced over at O'Brien, whom he hadn't met yet.

'I thought so, too,' Tate grumbled.

'Hey, there'a a cot made up back there. We got a prisoner coming in?'

'That's for O'Brien here,' Tate said. 'He's going to be our guest for a few nights.'

Webster looked O'Brien over with a frown. 'Well. What if we need that cot for a prisoner?'

'We won't need the damn cot!' Tate fairly shouted at him. 'Are them shotguns still locked up in that case back there?'

The frown returned to Webster's thin face. 'Sure.'

'Go get two of them, and make sure they're loaded.'

Jock looked over at O'Brien, suddenly very glad the buffalo hunter was there.

'Why do you want the shotguns?' Webster was saying in his reedy voice.

Tate turned to him, red-faced. 'Because Rabbit Purcell killed a man tonight!' he bellowed.

Webster's face fell into straight lines. 'Oh.'

'Now go get the damn guns,' Tate said heavily.

Webster turned and left them, heading down the short corridor to the rear, looking stunned. O'Brien sat on the corner of Tate's desk. 'I'm not sure this is such a good idea, Marshal.'

Tate was retrieving extra shotgun shells from a wall cabinet. 'This ain't your play, O'Brien. I'm the one wearing the badge.'

'I agree with O'Brien,' Jock put in quietly. His young cheeks were flushed, and he could feel his heart pummeling his chest.

Tate glanced at him impatiently. 'You stay here with O'Brien and watch the jail. Don't worry. I'm not about to do anything foolish. I'm not going there to arrest anybody. I'm going to get Purcell's oral statement about the way it all went down. It's expected of me.'

'This just happened this evening,' O'Brien persisted. 'No matter how calm

110

and reasonable you are, them men are still flushed with the heat of it all. It might not go as peaceably as you hope.'

Tate narrowed his eyes on O'Brien. 'I know that. But it's my job, nobody else's. I'll take Webster with me.'

'Webster?' Jock said. 'You'd be better off with me!'

Tate gave him an angry look. 'Don't be foolish, boy.'

'Nobody will expect you to go tonight,' O'Brien said quietly. He held Tate's gaze with a calm one. 'You can go tomorrow morning and get the same job done.'

Tate hesitated. Then Webster arrived with the guns. 'OK. I'm ready to go!'

O'Brien took one of the shotguns from him. 'Anyway, I'm walking over there. For a drink.' He spoke more slowly. 'By myself.'

Jock was regarding him breathlessly now. 'You?'

'Hey, what's going on here?' Webster asked.

O'Brien casually broke the big gun

open to check its ammo, then locked it back in place with a metallic clacking.

'Now, wait,' Tate protested weakly.

'I'll get a feel for things at the Schooner that might help you tomorrow morning.' He was avoiding Tate's eyes now.

'What are you thinking?' Tate asked suspiciously. 'Like I said, this is my play, O'Brien.'

'It's mine, too,' O'Brien said. 'Don't worry, I'm not getting involved in your little war. I couldn't care less. I'm just taking care of personal business.'

All three of them furrowed their brows at that. But then Jock understood. 'O'Brien. I don't want this. At least let one of us go with you.'

O'Brien pointed a finger at him. 'You stay put. You understand?'

Jock swallowed hard. He nodded. At that moment he was sorry he had written to O'Brien.

'Well, I'll just walk along with you,' Tate said.

'No. This is my play, Marshal.'

'What's going on around here?' Webster said.

But while they were all trying to assess what had happened in the past few minutes, O'Brien settled the long gun under his arm and left the building.

* * *

Over at the Prairie Schooner there was a celebration taking place. After the first shock of Purcell's rash action at the NPM meeting, with the death of Will St Clair, Luke Mallory was privately content with the way things had gone. The developments of the night had put a scare into the reformers that wouldn't be forgotten quickly. His only reservation about the new situation was that it was now very clear that R.C. Wilson and his little cadre of guns might just be more than Mallory could handle. Wilson was already talking about 'running the town' after they 'got rid of' Marshal Tate, and that kind of talk scared Mallory.

But tonight was a merry one at the Schooner. There had been a round of drinks on the house, and spirits were high and tongues loose.

'Did you see the look on his face when he saw he was beat?' Purcell was saying to his comrades at his table. Sitting with him were Wilson, Rueda and Mallory. Actually, though, Purcell had drunk very little because he thought it would impair his enjoyment of what had happened at the NPM meeting.

'Keep it down a little,' Mallory said, looking around. 'You never know who might be listening.'

'I don't care if the damn governor is listening.' Purcell grinned. 'I'm going to enjoy this!'

'Leave him be.' Wilson smiled. 'He's like a kid with a new pony.'

Rueda raised his glass of whiskey. 'To the death of NPM!' he shouted.

Mallory shook his head. Some cowpokes at a couple of nearby tables joined in noisily, repeating Rueda's toast. But then one man near the door, sitting by himself, stood up soberly.

'I don't like the NPM either. But I don't think we should be making fun of a man who just lost his life a couple hours ago.'

Purcell got a dark look on his pallid face, and started to rise, but Wilson stopped him. 'No. Let me.'

Wilson pushed his chair back and got up. Mallory sighed heavily. 'Is there something you want to do about it, dogie-lover?' Wilson said in a low, level voice. The lone man was a young cowhand from a nearby ranch. 'I see you're carrying iron. Let's see if you can use it to back up that saucy talk.'

The ranch hand looked scared, already wishing he had kept his silence. 'You're the fastest gun in Kansas, Wilson. I wasn't looking for no showdown. I'd just like to see a little respect for the dead.'

'So you're saying we're disrespectful?' Wilson persisted.

'Wilson,' Mallory said quietly. 'Not

again. Not tonight.'

Wilson didn't even acknowledge his remarks. 'I asked you a simple question, cow-pucky. I don't like to be ignored.'

The cowboy ran a hand across his mouth. 'I'm not drawing down on you, Wilson.'

'No?' Wilson smiled. 'Then I guess you're a dirty, low-down loudmouth yellow-belly then. You know what we do to yellow-bellies in the Schooner?'

In the next instant, Wilson drew the Enfield Mark II on his hip in a lightning-fast movement the eye could not follow, and the gun erupted in a cacophonous roaring that banged ear-drums and made glass rattle on the shelves behind the mahogany bar. In a slight crouch, Wilson fanned the revolver over and over as patrons watched wide-eyed. The hot slugs blew the cowboy's right ear-lobe off, then his left, then tore his hat from his head, and the last one severed his gun holster from its belt as it plummeted noisily to the floor.

It all happened in less than five seconds. As the smoke cleared, and the other patrons saw what had happened, laughter slowly erupted around the room, with Purcell and Rueda laughing the loudest.

The cowpoke stood there trembling, not sure he was still alive. His hands went to his ears, and came away with blood on them. He just stared at them for a long moment.

'Kill him!' Purcell yelled gaily.

The laughter subsided. Wilson twirled the Enfield forward three times, then backwards twice, in a swift, fluid motion, and let the weapon settle back into its holster. Somebody behind Wilson whistled softly between his teeth.

'He isn't worth killing,' Wilson said at last. 'Now get to hell out of here, boy. And don't come back.'

The assaulted cowboy looked at his right hand again, looked around the room sadly, then turned and left.

The only laughter then came from Purcell and Rueda.

Mallory gave Wilson a sidewise scowl, but Wilson didn't see it. He walked over to the bar, where Big Betty had just recovered from all the excitement.

'Did you have to do that?' she asked him.

Wilson back-handed her across her cheek, and made her jump in shock. She grabbed at her face, breathing hard. 'Damn you.'

'I'm going down to the Dogie. When I get back, I want you upstairs waiting for me. Be there.'

Betty didn't reply. Wilson turned then and, nodding to his table, left the saloon. Five minutes later, when the room had settled down again, Mallory got up to give his bartender some instructions. When he arrived behind the bar O'Brien walked in the door.

He caught the attention of most of those near the swinging doors immediately, including Rueda and Purcell. He was carrying the eight-gauge, single-shot Remington shotgun under his right arm. He rarely took his riding spurs off, and they clinked dully as he strode to an empty table not far from where Purcell and Rueda sat. Mallory turned and regarded him warily as O'Brien took a seat at the table, facing the two gunmen, and laid the long gun on the table beside him. He almost never carried any kind of sidearm, and the only weapon he had besides the shotgun was the skinning knife in his right stovepipe boot.

'Bring me a bottle of your best bust-head, double-rectified whiskey,' he said over his shoulder to the barkeep.

The bartender looked at Mallory, and Mallory nodded his approval. The bartender took the bottle out and deposited it and a shot glass on O'Brien's table. O'Brien threw some coins onto the table, and the other man picked them up and left. O'Brien poured out a glass and swigged it down.

'Hey, Mallory!' Purcell called out. 'You started serving stinking hide-men in here now? Some of us got sensitive noses, you know!'

Rueda really liked that. He burst out in raucous laughter. He was having a great evening. Several other patrons joined in, but a few already had a bad feeling about this big rawhide man.

'*Sí*, my *nanz* is *muy* sensitive!' Rueda chimed in. 'Maybe you could move him to the back wall!'

'What the hell are you doing in here, buffalo man?' Purcell went on. 'Thinking you can drink with civilized folks?'

O'Brien poured another glass of red-top rye. 'I came here to kill you,' he said in a quiet, even voice.

The entire room went deadly quiet in a moment. At the back of the place, a patron squinted toward O'Brien. 'What did he say?'

At Purcell's table, both he and Rueda stared in sudden sobriety at the buffalo hunter. 'What?' Purcell said ominously. 'What did you say?'

'I think you heard me,' O'Brien replied. 'You're the piece of shit that threatened Jock Sumner, ain't you?'

Purcell's hard, pink eyes narrowed down on O'Brien. 'I'll take that punk kid down any time now.' He rose from his chair, and stepped away from the table. His right hand went out over his Colt .45, a gun that could blow a hole right through a man. 'You want to do something about it?'

A customer near the line of fire jumped off his chair and stumbled out of harm's way. Over at the bar, Mallory had already had too much for one evening. 'Wait a minute, boys! There's no need for trouble here!'

'Shut up,' O'Brien said easily, without looking toward him. He had put his hand on the long gun, but was still seated at the table. 'I told you what I'm going to do about it.' His hand found the trigger assembly on the big gun.

Purcell's eyes went very wild in that moment, and O'Brien saw his hand go for the Colt. O'Brien raised the muzzle of the shotgun and squeezed the trigger, beating Purcell by a full second.

Nothing happened.

The hammer clicked dully on a dud cartridge that Tate had had in the gun for ever. O'Brien swore softly.

Purcell hadn't fired yet. His Colt was aimed at O'Brien's heart, but when he saw that O'Brien was now disarmed, he hesitated. Then he started laughing again, and Rueda joined in.

'Well, well!' Purcell purred. 'The big hunter with big ideas can't even keep himself in good ammo! Now who's going to die, big man?'

'Kill him!' Rueda yelled happily. 'Blow his liver out!'

Purcell didn't need a further invitation. He re-aimed the Colt at O'Brien's forehead, intending to put one right between his eyes. But O'Brien had slid his right leg back just slightly, and eased his hand to the Bowie which was just at arm's length. As Purcell's finger tightened over the trigger, O'Brien slid the big knife from its sheath and hurled it past his table at Purcell, all in one smooth, unobtrusive movement.

The knife flew through the air like a

striking cobra, turned over just once, and buried itself in Purcell's mid-chest.

Purcell's gun fired then, the lead grazing O'Brien's temple and making a bloody mark there. Purcell stood there looking down at the handle of the Bowie as if O'Brien had performed some kind of magic on him. He looked up at O'Brien with a puzzled expression, and his gun fired again, into the wood-plank floor, then Purcell fell forward on to his face, driving the knife into him to the hilt. The floor shook when he hit, then an eery silence fell into the room. Nobody moved. Nobody spoke.

O'Brien picked up his glass of whiskey, and downed it in one long gulp. 'That boy would scare crows out of a cornfield,' he said to himself.

Rueda now jumped off his chair, his face twitching. He drew his Joslyn .44 and aimed it at O'Brien. 'If he can't do it, I will, *por Dios!*' he hissed out.

O'Brien put the glass down. 'You shoot me with that, you Mex weasel, and I'll come over there and beat you to death with it.'

Something about the way he said it made Rueda hesitate. Out on the edge of town somewhere a coyote wailed into the night, like a warning. Mallory caught Rueda's eye and shook his head sideways. Rueda hesitated again, and then reholstered his gun.

O'Brien got up, went and bent over Purcell, and retrieved his knife. He wiped Purcell's blood off it onto Purcell's shirt, and replaced it in his boot. Then he picked up the shotgun again, and the bottle, and walked to the front entrance.

He turned back to Mallory. 'A word of advice. Don't water that whiskey so thin and you might sell more of it.'

Then he was gone out the door.

5

When O'Brien arrived back at the marshal's office, Tate had just grabbed a shotgun and was headed out the door to see what had happened to him.

Webster and Jock were also there up front, Jock looking very tense. A big grin moved his young face when O'Brien came through the door looking as if he had just taken a relaxing stroll.

'Oh, thank God,' Tate sighed. 'I was about to go looking for you.'

O'Brien gave him a sour look and set the whiskey bottle that he had carried from the saloon onto Tate's desk. 'Thought you might like the rest of this bottle. But it's about next to drinking well-water.'

They all watched him as he walked down the corridor to the gun case and set the shotgun in a rack. 'You ought to buy yourself some new cartridges for these guns, though. I went over there with a bad one.'

'Damn!' Jock muttered.

'I told you a couple of them shells had went soft,' Webster said with a self-satisfied grin.

'Jesus!' Tate grumbled. 'Hey. What happened over there? Did you get any trouble from Wilson or Purcell?'

'Purcell is dead,' O'Brien said. 'Did you make any coffee while I was gone?'

All three were staring hard at him. 'Dead?' Webster said in a sarcastic manner. 'What are you talking about? I just saw him earlier.'

Jock's face, though, had broken into a wider grin. 'You killed him.'

O'Brien just looked over at him briefly, then sat down on Tate's chair behind the old desk. 'I reckon I'll have to wait for that coffee.'

'I'll make some,' Jock said excitedly. He hadn't wanted to admit it to Tate, but he had been worried about Purcell being out there looking for him. 'But tell us what happened.'

'Yes,' Tate said deliberately. 'What the hell happened over there?'

O'Brien met his sober gaze. 'You don't have to arrest me, Marshal. He made the first move. You can ask anybody who was there.'

'I just saw him earlier!' Webster protested.

'Shut up, Webster,' Tate said. He sat on the edge of his desk facing O'Brien. 'Purcell? Dead?'

'That's right,' Jock said proudly.

'That's why you went over there,' Tate said.

O'Brien just sat there. 'Are you going to make that coffee or not, kid?' he said to Jock.

Webster frowned. 'You seem like an ornery bastard.'

'Shut up, Webster,' Jock said quietly. Then he went to make the coffee, his head still spinning with the news.

'Hey!' Webster said after him.

'Will Mallory be making charges against you?' Tate asked O'Brien.

'He ain't the type to make charges,' O'Brien said.

'They may come after you,' Tate said. 'You might have started a war tonight.'

O'Brien regarded him soberly. 'You already had a war, Marshal. You just been ignoring it.'

Tate hesitated. 'I know. The fact is, I just ain't cut out to keep the peace in a situation like this. I never been up against real killers before. I just don't know where it's all going to lead.' He paused again. 'But thanks, O'Brien. Purcell might have been the worst of them.'

'Look,' O'Brien said. 'If your mayor don't back you, you have a good excuse to take that badge off and let somebody else take it. Tell Jock to go back out to that ranch where he was working before. Get him away from all this. If the reformers want to civilize this town, let them decide how much of this they want.'

'If I turn this badge in R.C. Wilson will run this town,' Tate said slowly.

O'Brien shrugged. 'Then it will be up to the town to take it back.'

Jock arrived then with a tin cup of steaming hot coffee, and delivered it to O'Brien. O'Brien gave him a slight grin and took a long swig of the boiling hot liquid, to Jock's amazement.

'I been meaning to take you out hunting while I'm here,' O'Brien said to him. 'How about tomorrow morning?'

'That would be just great.' Jock grinned.

'All the small game's been cleaned out around here for miles around,' Webster said. Then when Jock gave him a hard look, he turned and headed down the corridor.

'He just don't know any better,' Tate said.

A few minutes later, he and Jock had left for home, leaving Webster on duty and O'Brien to find some well-deserved rest for the night.

★ ★ ★

The following morning O'Brien was up at dawn. Jock came into town soon thereafter and after a quick breakfast they rode out together.

It was a beautiful spring morning. Wildflowers had erupted onto the plains, and the redolence of them was carried on a soft breeze.

In the first hour they had shot three guinea hens, a partridge, and a silver fox, with O'Brien allowing Jock to do most of the shooting. Then, when they crested a low ridge flanked by cottonwoods, O'Brien reined in sharply. He squinted into the distance.

Jock saw nothing. 'What is it?' he asked.

'Buffalo. It's just a speck out there.' He pointed. 'See him?'

Jock squinted too, and saw it. They spurred their mounts forward, closing the distance slowly. The speck grew larger until they were within about 500 yards. O'Brien dismounted and Jock followed.

'Take the Sharps out of the scabbard,' O'Brien told him.

Jock was very excited. He had only handled the Sharps one other time, on O'Brien's only other visit. He slid the heavy gun out, and its tripod.

'Set it up right here,' O'Brien said.

Jock followed orders. In moments the Sharps was ready. O'Brien knelt behind the gun, and found the bull buffalo in his sights. He turned to Jock.

'What do you think?'

Jock shook his head. 'I'm no good at long shooting yet. You take him.'

'Are you sure?'

'Yeah. I'd ruin it for us. Please. You shoot.'

O'Brien nodded, grabbed the long gun and sighted in again. The buffalo was actually moving a little closer. O'Brien narrowed his eyes on the animal, and shook his head. 'I'll be damned.'

'What is it?'

He was studying the great bulk of the buffalo, and the quality of its coat. 'It's the same bull,' he said slowly. 'I saw him on my way to Sulphur Creek. He was in a herd with a handful of other shaggies. There was a thunderstorm and I missed my chance at him.'

He looked over at Jock. 'The rest of the herd scattered west. They must be halfway to the mountains by now. But he stayed behind.'

'Great,' Jock said. 'You get a second chance!'

O'Brien stared out over the gun to the buffalo. *That must be the last damn buffalo in this whole territory*, he said to himself.

Jock noticed the change that had come over O'Brien, and frowned slightly. O'Brien sighted the animal in once more, and put the crosshairs right on the buffalo's nose. Then the buffalo turned its shaggy head and looked right at him.

It was an easy shot for O'Brien. He had made that shot over and over again in his many years of hunting. His finger snugged down on the trigger.

He hesitated. Maybe it was because that beautiful animal was out there on the plains all by itself, defying the world, challenging the relentless winds of change that were sweeping over the land.

He released his grip on the trigger, and let a long breath out. Then he aimed the muzzle of the gun above the buffalo's head, and fired.

The animal started, then bolted off across the long grass and wildflowers until it disappeared over a low hill.

Jock turned to O'Brien, his mouth slightly open. 'You did that on purpose. You let it run.'

O'Brien rose to his feet, not looking at Jock. 'Put the damn Sharps back on the Appaloosa. I reckon we had enough of this for the day.'

Jock thought he understood. 'Sure, O'Brien. When we get back, I'll pluck one of the guinea hens for supper.'

O'Brien came and stood beside Jock while he slid the Sharps back into its saddle scabbard. 'That fight in town ain't yours,' he said. 'I'll be leaving here tomorrow. And I'd like to think you got sense enough to take care of yourself.'

Jock was touched by that. 'I will, O'Brien.'

O'Brien stared at the boy's young, pink-cheeked face and found himself wondering if he had ever been so innocent. In that moment he came to a shocking realization. He actually cared for somebody.

He punched Jock lightly on the arm, and Jock briefly felt the raw power behind that friendly gesture. 'Come on, kid. The marshal will be watching for us.'

★ ★ ★

In town at the Prairie Schooner the atmosphere wasn't as peaceable. With Rabbit Purcell's corpse warming a slab at the undertaker's alongside the man he had killed, things weren't looking as rosy for the so-called Peace Commission as they had just yesterday.

Mallory had closed the saloon down

temporarily while their present circumstances were being discussed, and they
were all gathered in the big bar room
where customers usually drank Mallory's liquor. All except Maynard
McComb, who had left town. They
were all seated around the room in a
loose cluster, looking sober.

'Everything was fine around here,'
Mallory was saying. 'Then this damned
wild man shows up and kills Purcell.'

Sitting near Mallory with Rueda,
Wilson grunted. 'If Tate wasn't over
there, acting like a marshal, none of this
would have happened.'

'Tate probably deputized the hunter,'
Rueda offered in his thick accent. He
was still embarrassed because he had
had a clear opportunity to kill O'Brien
and had hesitated.

Hank Logan, the owner of the Dogie,
seemed jumpy. 'McComb knew all
about this O'Brien. From up in
Montana. He came here just to see that
damned Sumner kid.'

Mallory's face changed. 'Of course.

And Purcell had threatened the kid's life. It was all about the kid.'

'That's it,' Logan said tightly, fidgeting on his chair.

'But that makes one more to deal with,' Wilson said. 'I'm telling you, Mallory. It's time to take some action on this. Rabbit's death just may give the reformers some backbone and swing the town on to their side. We can begin with Tate. With him gone, that lame-brain Webster will run or hide, and that hunter will ride out. He has no interest in this town. If he doesn't leave, I'll send him to hell with Rabbit.' He gave a small grin.

'You're all taking this pretty light,' Logan said, sitting in a far corner. He had looked tense since McComb left him. A tic moved the edge of his face. 'I have a bad feeling about all this, damn it.'

Mallory squinted down on him. 'Have you been drinking, Hank?'

Logan wiped a hand across his mouth. 'Just a couple of ryes. It's just that . . . well, first there's that loud-mouth kid. He's in tight with Nell Douglas and Hawkins, you know.' He paused. 'That no-good uncle of his hoorawed me once in Dodge.' The tic twitched again. 'The kid will be just like him. And now we have this O'Brien. Close to him as turkeys in a pen. It's a dangerous combination, I tell you.'

Wilson regarded him soberly. But it was Mallory who spoke.

'You're not going to have a nervous breakdown on me now, are you, Hank?'

Rueda laughed to himself, enjoying Logan's new weakness.

Logan's face had gone red. 'Goddam it, you don't get it! There's stories about this O'Brien you wouldn't believe.'

'Then don't believe them,' Wilson said.

'I know things get exaggerated. But if they're just partly true, he's trouble. Him and that kid. He rode with Certainty Sumner, you know. That's why he and the kid are so close.'

Mallory was studying Logan's flushed

face. 'If you're not up to all this, Hank, maybe you better close up the Dogie and bow out for a while.'

'You might feel safer away from here.' Wilson smiled.

Logan rose from his chair, huffing. 'Are you calling me a coward, damn you! You think I'm afraid to use a gun?'

'Nobody called you a coward,' Mallory said to him.

'You'll see! When the time comes to act. I'll be there! Just like the rest of you!'

'Sit down, Hank,' Mallory said.

'I have things to do at the Dogie,' Logan said bitterly. 'I'll see you all later.'

A few moments later, when he was gone, Wilson turned to Mallory. 'That boy will be worthless to us.'

'He is going loco in the head.' Rueda laughed. 'I have seen it before.'

'I just hope he doesn't do something stupid,' Mallory suggested. 'I've known Hank forever, and I've never seen him act like that.'

'We don't need him,' Wilson said. 'We'll proceed like we discussed. Scare Tate out of town, or ride him out on a rail. I'll take him out if you prefer.'

Mallory sighed. 'Let me think on this. We'll talk later.'

* * *

When O'Brien and Jock returned from their morning hunt Tate was at the jail alone. After cleaning the shot birds and skinning the fox they all walked down to the Frontier Hotel and ate lunch in its dining room. When they had finished eating, and were still drinking refilled coffee, Tate looked over at O'Brien, who was bare-headed and wild-looking.

'Jock said you was thinking of riding out tomorrow.'

O'Brien nodded, and took a swig of hot coffee. 'I'm on my way into the Indian Territory. It's one of the wild places left out here. If your reformers showed up down there they'd end up hanging from a mesquite tree.'

Tate regarded him studiedly. 'You sound like that wouldn't bother you much.'

Jock wasn't drinking coffee. He gave Tate a took, then glanced over at O'Brien.

O'Brien shrugged. 'I'm not sure closing saloons down and putting up more churches is going to make the West a better place.'

'It will come eventually,' Tate said. 'Everything will change.'

'I don't want to be here when it does,' O'Brien said.

Tate set his coffee cup down and stared at his empty plate. A waiter came over to them in that silence, and smiled at Tate. 'Well, Marshal. Anything else I can get for you boys?'

'No, I reckon not. But I'll take that check when it's ready.'

O'Brien frowned slightly at that, as the waiter nodded and left.

Tate caught his eye. 'Look, O'Brien. I like the way you do things. You could be a big help to us right now. You see what

Webster is. It's like not having a deputy at all. Would you consider staying on here for a short spell? I could pin a badge on you and have me a real man beside me. Just till this saloon thing sorts itself out.'

O'Brien's frown deepened. 'Marshal, I don't mean to throw mud on nobody here, but that's the worst idea I've heard in some time. I never wore a badge in my life and never will. I'm a hunter. That's all I know. And I don't care whether the saloons or the reformers run this town.'

Jock was frowning, too. 'O'Brien has his own life to lead, Uriah. We can't ask him to get involved in our problems here.'

Tate sighed. 'You're right. I'm sorry, O'Brien. I shouldn't have asked. I guess I was just looking forward to seeing the looks on Mallory's and Logan's faces when they saw a badge on your chest.'

'No offense taken,' O'Brien told him. 'But I think you should keep Jock here as far from all this as you can.'

'I will,' Tate replied quietly.

Jock felt warm inside whenever O'Brien expressed an interest in his welfare. He still found it hard to believe O'Brien had killed Rabbit Purcell because of him. 'We'll both be OK,' he said to O'Brien. 'We're not afraid of Mallory and Logan.'

'Who's Logan?' O'Brien asked, remembering the name of the lawman he had had to kill in Colorado.

'He owns the other saloon,' Tate said. 'The Lost Dogie.'

'Any relatives in Colorado?'

'Why, yes. I think he has a cousin there. A marshal up at Birney Pass. You know him?'

'I just met him in passing,' O'Brien said. He still had healing wounds from that encounter and the earlier one with the bear, and the cut on his right cheek from the bear still showed a raw scar, but Tate and Jock were too polite to ask about it. The grazing one from Purcell was scabbing over but hidden by his wild hair.

'I reckon that whole family tree went bad,' Tate surmised.

At that moment the front door opened and R.C. Wilson walked in. He was all in black, with a yellow kerchief at his neck. He wore a flat-top, wide-brim Stetson that was also black. His Enfield looked like a cannon on his hip.

He didn't see their table immediately. He walked over to the cash register where the waiter was counting change. 'Me and a friend will be coming in tonight for sirloins. You got plenty back there?'

The waiter looked suddenly scared. 'Oh, yes sir, Mr Wilson. Any time you want them, we got them here. I'll put two big ones aside for you. Anything else I can do?'

'Just have those steaks ready to fry up,' Wilson said curtly. 'And I don't want them like shoe leather this time.'

'Oh, no sir,' the waiter replied. 'We'll make them any way you want.'

When Wilson turned to leave, he saw

who was sitting at the nearby table. 'Well, well. If it isn't our town marshal.'

He came over and smiled at Tate, then looked O'Brien over carefully.

Tate nodded. 'Wilson. I was hoping you'd left town.'

Wilson laughed softly. 'No, no, Marshal. I've gotten to like this little cow flop of a town you got here. Why, I might be here longer than you!'

They all looked up at him soberly, not missing the implications of that remark. 'Oh, I doubt that, Wilson,' Tate said.

'I doubt you'll be here long at all,' Jock said emotionally.

Wilson gave him a somber look. 'I see you're letting kids do your talking for you. You aim to let him do your fighting, too, Marshal?'

Tate remained calm. 'We let our kids speak their minds in this town, mister. And we can do our own fighting.'

'I guess that remains to be seen,' Wilson said pointedly. He looked over at O'Brien again. 'I don't think I've met your new friend here.'

Tate glanced over at O'Brien. 'This is O'Brien. But I think you probably already know that. He's here visiting Jock. Any objections?'

'None at all,' Wilson said, facing O'Brien directly. 'So you're the man who murdered Rabbit Purcell.'

O'Brien glanced up at him irritably. 'If you was there, you'd know it wasn't murder. If that's any of your business.'

'I count it my business,' Wilson said, the grin gone. 'Purcell was my friend.'

O'Brien took a last swig of coffee. 'Then you must have dung beetles for friends.'

Tate and Jock saw Wilson's face cloud over. He leaned over the table toward O'Brien. 'You've got a big mouth for a man that's not carrying,' he said in a quiet, menacing tone.

O'Brien hadn't brought his Winchester rifle to the hotel, and felt a bit naked without it. He looked up at Wilson again. He had always had a severe dislike of gunfighters and especially those who hired their guns out to kill other men they had never met.

'If you're through showing that Mark II off to the room, maybe you'll let us finish our coffee in peace here.'

Jock laughed quietly at that, and Wilson turned a hot look on him before addressing O'Brien again.

'If I'd been in the saloon that day, you'd be a dead man now,' he growled at O'Brien.

'Or you would!' Jock cried out, his cheeks ablaze.

Wilson gave him a blistering look. 'I see why Rabbit wanted your skin, you little snake! I'm beginning to feel the same way!'

O'Brien turned a slow look on him, then rose from his chair. He was suddenly toe to toe with Wilson, and nose to nose. He stood about an inch taller than Wilson, and was much broader. For the first time Wilson felt what so many others had felt when in close proximity to the hunter.

'You're beginning to get into my

craw,' he said in Wilson's face. 'Why don't you just get to hell out of here while you can?'

Wilson was breathless with surprise and anger. Nobody ever talked to him like that and lived to tell about it. 'Why, you stupid hide-stripper! I could shoot you down in the next second and shut you up for good!'

'Could you?' O'Brien said. 'Why don't you give it a try and see how it all works out?'

'No, wait!' Tate yelled. 'There's no cause for that.' He still had no understanding of O'Brien's capability, and he was very scared.

Jock sat there breathless, also scared.

Wilson's right hand went out over the Enfield, but he paused there. The big hunter was within inches of him, and could interfere with his draw. Anything could happen. He forced a smile onto his aquiline face and let his hand drop back down to his thigh.

'This isn't the proper place,' he said. 'Or time.'

'You mean because I'm facing you?' O'Brien grated out.

There was a slight flush on Wilson's face again, but he controlled his reaction. 'They told me it was you I'd have to deal with,' he said quietly. 'Well, I have a friendly warning for you, buffalo man. I understand you're just passing through Sulphur Creek. I'd suggest you get on your mount and ride out of here as fast as it will carry you. Is that simple enough for you to understand?'

'I told you to leave, and you're still here,' O'Brien said darkly.

Wilson tried an arrogant grin. 'Good day, gentlemen.'

When he had disappeared through the door Tate blew his cheeks out. 'Thank God. I thought sure he'd kill you.'

'He wouldn't have killed O'Brien,' Jock said, still breathing hard.

O'Brien sat back down. His square face was very somber. He hadn't liked the new threat against Jock. 'He was crowded for space,' he said. 'It wasn't a sure thing for him, and Wilson likes a sure thing. Like most gunslingers for hire.'

'You would have killed him,' Jock said.

Tate looked over at him, and saw the admiration in his young eyes. He turned to O'Brien. 'I reckon what he said was a lot of bluster, O'Brien. He's mad about Purcell. Just ignore him.'

'It wasn't bluster,' O'Brien said. 'Wilson is running the show over there now. Mallory has lost control.'

'He'll have to come through me,' Tate said grimly.

'That's what I'm afraid of,' O'Brien countered.

Tate frowned slightly. 'I know what I'm in for. But I took an oath when I pinned this badge on. The law says the saloons have to be closed down, and I was sworn in to uphold the law. Them NPM people aren't going away, and they expect me to act for them. I just have to find a way to do it.'

'It's beyond saloon closing,' O'Brien said. 'Wilson and that Mexican want to own this town. Defending the saloons is just an excuse for getting rid of you and the law.'

'Well,' Tate said. 'I'm not getting out of their way. It's not just about the NPM. A lot of townfolks expect me to stand up to them. Even if that makes me a target.'

O'Brien had expected that kind of reply. He sighed. 'Well. Then we have to start watching our backs.'

'We?' Jock exclaimed.

'Wilson just made this my business again. I'll stick around a little while, just to see how things go.'

'Are you sure?' Tate said hopefully.

O'Brien just looked at him. 'Why don't we get back down to the jail? Webster might've set it on fire by now.'

6

Uriah Tate felt a lot better about the situation in Sulphur Creek since O'Brien's decision to stay on for a while. He had felt very alone in the growing conflict before that, despite having Jock and Webster at his side.

When they returned to Tate's office Webster was asleep in one of the cells in the rear. Tate made them some more coffee because he thought the stuff at the hotel tasted a lot like 'cow piss'. He, O'Brien and Jock all sat around the office then, drinking Tate's coffee from tin cups. O'Brien and Tate were at Tate's desk, and Jock occupied a stool in a corner.

'So Logan's hired gun just rode out?' O'Brien was saying.

Tate nodded. 'McComb was always different from these others. He's no born killer. I don't think he liked what happened at that NPM meeting, with St Clair ending up dead.'

'That's not necessarily good,' O'Brien commented. 'The rest of them are probably all of the same mind now.'

'Too bad McComb left,' Jock offered. 'He wasn't a bad guy.'

O'Brien caught his eye and returned an easy smile. The kid was definitely worth taking some time to look after. He was about to speak to Tate again, when the front door burst open and several people blustered in.

Those in first were NPM people: Avery Hawkins, their chairman; Ned Tanner, Hawkins's right-hand man; Nell Douglas the WCTU woman; and two other members whose names Tate didn't know. Behind them were four irate townsfolk, supporters of the reform movement.

Tate frowned, and slid his feet off his desk. 'Well, well. What do we have here, Avery? A lynching party?'

There had been some talking among the newcomers upon arrival, but that noise now subsided. Hawkins cleared his throat.

'If you don't know why we're here, Marshal, you damn well should!' Hawkins began. He glanced over at O'Brien, sitting beside Tate's desk, and then turned back to Tate. 'We're here to demand action, by God!'

'Watch your language, Avery,' Nell Douglas told him severely.

Hawkins eyed her impatiently, without responding. 'What do you have to say for yourself, Marshal? When I rode out to your cabin after St Clair was viciously murdered, you assured me you would take care of matters. But nothing has been done. Oh, we know that Purcell was served his just deserts by some trail bum. But that hasn't changed anything at the saloons.'

'It wasn't a trail bum that killed Purcell. It was this fellow here. This is O'Brien. He's a friend of Jock, and Jock's deceased uncle.'

They all looked at O'Brien. 'We don't sanction killing as a means to achieve desired results,' Nell Douglas spoke up again. 'He who lives by the sword shall die by the sword.'

'Please, Nell,' Hawkins admonished her.

'A friend of Certainty Sumner?' Tanner said. 'What did you do, Tate? Bring in your own hired gun?'

'If he did, it's OK with me!' called a local man from the rear of the group. 'Something has to be done by someone! Before they kill again to protect their foul places of business!'

'That's right!' another supporter boomed out.

'What's the matter with you people?' Jock suddenly blurted out. 'The marshal is doing his best with what he has!'

'When we arrived here, we asked you to uphold the state law and close your saloons down,' Hawkins went on. 'You said they're still open in Dodge City, and other places. But we want to set an example here. You asked us to compromise by accepting dismissal of the saloon prostitutes, and we OK'd that as a temporary solution. But you haven't even done that.'

'I demanded their resignation,' Tate said. 'They wanted some more time. You can't be arbitrary about these things.'

'Well, the town is in back of us now, Marshal. And most are past wanting the girls fired. People are talking about burning the saloons to the ground!'

'I'm for that!' a local man called out. 'Get rid of them once and for all! Then men like Mallory and Logan will leave us to our town!'

'We don't want violence, gentlemen,' Nell Douglas said weakly.

'Do you see what I mean?' Hawkins said to Tate. 'Our supporters are arming themselves. I can't control this, Tate! This could all end in a damn bloodbath! And it will be on your head!'

O'Brien rose from his chair near Tate, went to a small wood stove nearby and poured his coffee grounds into its pot belly. Everybody quieted down in those moments and watched his every move. He was an unknown factor in their situation. After a while he turned back to them.

'Frankly, I can't imagine why this man sticks his neck out for you bunch of crazy Bible-thumpers.'

Hawkins's eyes narrowed on this tough-looking man in the rawhide clothes. Nell gasped quietly, and clutched a prayer book to her bosom. 'Why, you're a God-less man like the rest of them!'

'The hell he is!' Jock protested. 'He just doesn't believe in telling other folks how to run their lives!'

O'Brien looked over at him. 'It's all right, kid.'

'You're all damn lucky to have O'Brien here,' Tate said. 'He's the only one who's stood up to their guns.'

'If you folks like Boston ways a lot better than these out here, it might be better if you stayed back East,' O'Brien concluded. 'And not come here to cause all this commotion. It boils the blood and gives a man indigestion.'

Hawkins and the others just stared

hard at the hunter for a moment. Then Hawkins spoke again. 'Maybe you better not count on that one for any help,' he said soberly. 'I don't think he understands our mission.'

'If you're not with us, you're against us!' Ned Tanner exclaimed.

O'Brien shook his head, and turned to Tate. 'If you need me, I'll be back there cleaning the Winchester.' Then he walked on back to the cells.

Tate rose from his chair. 'All right, everybody. Let's all just calm down. I have every intention of following up on the girls. All of you just go back home and let the law work.'

'We told you!' the first local man said loudly. 'That ain't good enough now. Close the saloons or we'll close them! And we're not afraid of their hired thugs!'

Tate sighed. 'One step at a time, boys. I'm on your side. But you have to let me work this my way. No vigilante stuff. I couldn't help you if you break the law.'

'Just do something,' Hawkins said, pointing his finger at Tate. 'Or we will.'

They left then, with Nell Douglas muttering a prayer as she passed through the open door.

That evening and the following day passed peaceably. Tate was making plans in his head for returning to the Prairie Schooner to arrest Big Betty and Nita Ruiz, but he had to do it right, and without violence.

That was a big order.

Tate made a few street patrols in the meantime, day and night, and O'Brien decided to accompany him on these forays; Jock was allowed to go in the daylight. O'Brien carried his rifle on those rounds. He explained to Tate that he just needed the exercise, but Tate knew O'Brien had appointed himself as unofficial bodyguard to both himself and Jock.

O'Brien had made it clear previously that he thought Tate should keep out of the developing war. But this was the marshal's town, and O'Brien knew he wouldn't abandon it to men like Wilson and Mallory. So, in the end, O'Brien developed a grudging admiration for this ill-equipped upholder of the law.

On that next afternoon after the NPM descent on his office, Uriah Tate resolved to challenge the opposition on the following morning. O'Brien volunteered to join him. Jock pleaded for an hour to be allowed to go with them, but without success.

That evening Tate made his rounds of the city again, with O'Brien at his side. They paid particular attention to their surroundings as they passed the Schooner, and then the Lost Dogie.

'Wilson and that Mex ain't above back-shooting us in the dark,' O'Brien said as they passed the Dogie. As at the Schooner, music and other noise came from inside. Saloon patrons now were mostly cowboys and ranch hands from nearby ranches. Men from town mostly stayed away, with their wives backing the NPM and Nell Douglas.

As they passed an alleyway between

the Dogie and a general store, O'Brien put a hand on Tate's arm to stop him. 'Wait,' he said quietly, looking through the alley to the blackness behind the buildings. 'I thought I saw something.'

Tate squinted past him. 'I don't see nothing.'

But O'Brien stood and watched. In another moment, there was a brief flicker of light back there. 'There,' O'Brien said. 'Maybe you ought to check that out.'

Tate nodded, seeing the flicker of light again. They walked quickly through the alley to its end, and when they came out behind the buildings, they saw him. A dark figure behind the Dogie, holding a torch he had just lighted. He looked toward them in surprise. It was one of the men who had spoken up so angrily at the jail two days ago. Tate recognized him as a clerk in a local gun store.

'Jenkins!' Tate yelled. 'What the hell are you up to?'

Jenkins collected himself. 'What do

you think, Marshal! We told you what had to be done! Stand back, you can't stop me!'

He was very close to the building. There was a stink of kerosene in the air, and a can beside him on the ground. He picked the can up now. 'Just keep away, and you won't get hurt!'

'For God's sake, Jenkins! Don't you know there are still people inside? Just think a minute. Here, let me take that brand.'

Tate took a step toward Jenkins, and Jenkins threw some contents of the can toward him and O'Brien. The stuff ran along the ground right to their feet.

'I'll torch you if you try to stop this!' His eyes were glittery, his cheeks flushed. 'This is going to happen, Marshal!'

Tate stood there, frozen with renewed tension, looking at the wet ground between them. 'Please, Jenkins!'

O'Brien sighed and headed toward Jenkins, the rifle under his arm. 'That kerosene leads to you, too, you dimwit,' he growled.

'Stay back!' Jenkins cried hysterically. 'I'll fry you to a crisp, by God!'

O'Brien kept on toward him. Ten feet away. Five. Jenkins hesitated, looked at the ground. O'Brien swung the muzzle of the Winchester in a wide arc and hit Jenkins on his left cheek, shattering his jaw and busting most of his teeth on that side of his mouth. As he fell, O'Brien grabbed the torch and kept it from hitting the ground.

Jenkins hit the ground hard then, screaming in pain and holding his jaw. O'Brien threw the torch at a small well nearby; it disappeared inside and fizzled out in the watery depths.

Jenkins was spitting teeth out now, and blood. 'You — broke my jaw!' he whimpered in a muffled, broken voice.

Tate was still standing in the same place, trying to comprehend what had happened. O'Brien scuffed some dirt over the wet area where the kerosene had been thrown, as Tate walked over to Jenkins.

'How the hell did you do that?' he

said breathlessly to O'Brien.

O'Brien didn't respond to that. He never answered silly questions. 'You handcuff him and take him on down to the jail. I'm going to check out behind the Schooner.'

Then he turned and walked away, with Jenkins still moaning on the ground and Tate staring after him as if he had just really seen him for the first time.

* * *

By the next morning Jenkins had received medical help. Some broken teeth had been removed, and his jaw had been wired temporarily shut. A couple of townsfolk had seen Jenkins's removal to the jail, and word got back to Hawkins by early morning. By the time Tate was making up a pot of coffee Hawkins was there to see Jenkins. O'Brien was in the next cell, making his cot up. He never spoke to or looked at Hawkins.

Jenkins complained as loudly as he could of police brutality, and when Hawkins confronted Tate a few minutes later, he eyed Tate warily.

'What happened to Jenkins last night? He looks like a gut-wagon rolled over him.'

'He threatened O'Brien with a torch,' Tate said with a half-grin.

He was doing some paperwork at his desk, before heading over to the Prairie Schooner to arrest the saloon girls there. He expected to go to the Lost Dogie in the afternoon, to take Rose Nicely in too, even though she was a favorite of Mayor Provost. Webster was a few feet away, tacking a wanted dodger up on the bulletin board. He turned to Tate now.

'I don't know why you took him out with you. I'm the deputy here, by Jesus!'

They both ignored him. 'Jenkins says he's suing the city,' Hawkins went on. 'I know he went a little crazy last night. But I think he has a point.'

Tate leaned back on his chair. 'Are you sure you didn't encourage him in this, Hawkins? If you did, you're as guilty as he is.'

'I never approved arson or killing as a way to get the saloons closed,' Hawkins replied. 'You know that, Marshal.'

'I don't know what I know these days,' Tate said. 'But until I find any evidence against you, I'll still be behind NPM. I plan a visit down the street shortly, to get them girls headed out of town.'

'You want a couple of us to go with you?'

Tate shook his head. 'No, thanks. The situation will be volatile enough as it is. I'll give you a full report on it later.'

'We're both going,' Webster said from the bulletin board.

Hawkins grunted. 'I hope you're not taking that wild man too.'

Tate smiled. 'I reckon that's up to him.'

'We don't want any unnecessary violence,' Hawkins said. 'That can come back on all of us eventually.'

'Why don't you tell Jenkins that?' Tate replied sourly.

O'Brien had finished up back at his cell, and now came down the corridor toward them. When Jenkins saw him, he turned to the door. 'We'll expect to hear from you, Marshal.' He departed quickly.

Webster was watching O'Brien's arrival soberly, too. He gave O'Brien an acid look. 'How long are you going to be here?'

O'Brien ignored the question. Webster had never said anything to him that was worth responding to. He poured himself a tin cup of hot coffee and sat on the edge of Tate's desk. 'Did you leave Jock out at the cabin?'

Tate nodded. 'He's doing some housekeeping out there. I wanted to keep him out of town this morning.'

'You getting ready to visit the saloons?' He swigged the coffee.

'I'm just about set. You finished with that board, Webster?'

Webster came over to the desk. 'I'm ready to leave.' He looked thin and rheumy-eyed, and his vest bore an old gravy stain. He always looked like he had just gotten up from sleeping with his clothes on. He glanced over at O'Brien. 'We don't need you. We do this kind of stuff all the time.'

'For Christ's sake, Webster,' Tate grumbled.

'I'll just walk along,' O'Brien said. 'I hear Mallory gives away free boiled eggs with his watered beer. I might give it a try.'

'Why don't you wait till later?' Webster complained. He was sure O'Brien was a threat to his job with Tate. 'We got serious business to get done today.'

O'Brien turned to him casually, grabbed him by his shirt, and slammed him up against the wall beside the bulletin board. He pulled Webster up to his height, to speak face to face with him, and Webster's feet were pulled off the floor, dangling in mid-air.

'Your mouth is as sour as the smell of you. Keep it shut, or I'll have to hurt you,' he gritted in a quiet, hard voice.

Webster was gasping out his sudden terror, his jaw working without making any noise. At last, in a rush, he croaked, 'Let me go.'

O'Brien let him sag to the floor, breathless and pale. Then he turned to the marshal. 'I'm ready when you are.'

Tate was smiling slightly, trying to hide it from Webster. He rose from his desk, and came around it. 'Ready.' He looked over to Webster, who looked very shaken, and was eyeing O'Brien darkly. 'Are you still going, Webster?'

Webster found his voice. 'You going to let him do that to me?'

'From where I stand, you been asking for it,' Tate said. 'We're heading out, if you're coming.'

Webster hesitated, getting his wits back. 'I'm coming.' He aimed another dark look at O'Brien.

Then the three of them left for the Prairie Schooner.

It was already mid-morning when they arrived at the saloon. It was rather quiet inside, with just a handful of patrons. Luke Mallory was in a back office counting the last evening's receipts. R.C. Wilson was still upstairs in bed, and Rueda was cleaning up in a washroom beside Mallory's office. In the bar room with the patrons were the bartender and one of the saloon girls, Nita Ruiz. Nita was a good-looking, dark-haired Latina whom Rueda patronized regularly. She was leaning on the mahogany bar talking to the heavy bartender. When the three walked in, she and the barkeep stopped talking and the few patrons all turned to look at them. Tate walked over to Nita.

'There's a stage coming through in a few minutes, Nita. I want you on it.'

She gave him a disdainful look. 'Like hell!'

Tate sighed. 'Cuff her, Webster.'

Webster went to her and grabbed her arm; she tried to jerk away. 'Hey! You got no right to do this. Luke? Wilson?'

But Webster got her cuffed despite her struggles. She was fuming as she glanced over at O'Brien, who stood nearby with his Winchester under his arm. 'You think he makes a difference? He's already a dead man!'

'Where's Betty?' Tate asked nicely.

'None of your business,' Nita spat out.

'Does somebody want me?' It was Big Betty, coming down the staircase at the end of the room. She hadn't seen the cuffs on Nita.

'Get Luke,' Nita cried out. 'This moron is here trying to arrest us again.'

Betty was at the bottom of the stairs. Tate went over to her and slipped another pair of handcuffs on her before she figured out what he was doing.

'What do you think you're doing, Tate? You can't get away with this. Hey, Luke!' She spoke in an even louder voice than Nita's.

'It's almost time for the stage,' O'Brien said quietly, looking ominous standing there.

'You again!' Betty hissed at him, seeing him for the first time. Her face changed subtly. She had seen O'Brien kill Rabbit Purcell as she entered the room from Mallory's office that day.

Just at that moment Luke Mallory entered the room, with Pedro Rueda just behind him. They both stopped and stared as they assessed the situation. When Rueda saw O'Brien his eyes narrowed to slits.

'Goddam *cabron*!' he muttered. '*Regresa aqui?*'

'What's going on here, Marshal?' Mallory said slowly, also glancing at the buffalo hunter. He was now wearing a Smith & Wesson .32 revolver on his hip, and was considered quite good with it.

'This shouldn't surprise you, Mallory,' Tate said. 'I been telling you the girls have to go. We're just trying to keep your saloon from getting burnt down. But no need to thank us.'

'I'll thank you to take those cuffs off my girls,' Mallory said.

'Get these things off us, Luke!' Nita

171

complained loudly.

'These girls are walking across the street and getting on the stage that will pull up there in a few minutes,' Tate said. 'With them gone, I might just be able to derail a real war here, Mallory. The NPM people are arming themselves. This might just quiet them down.'

'We've decided we don't want any compromise solutions, Marshal. We want things just like they are. We'll take care of the reformers.'

'Well, I'm taking the girls,' Tate said resolutely. 'Webster.'

Webster jerked Nita toward the entrance, and Tate grabbed Betty again. But then Mallory drew his gun and aimed it at Tate. 'Stay where you are, girls.'

Webster stopped and turned. '*Idiota!*' Nita muttered.

Rueda eyed O'Brien, and started to draw his Joslyn.

'I wouldn't,' O'Brien said in a soft voice.

172

As he had when O'Brien killed Purcell, Rueda hesitated, then changed his mind. Mallory noted his uncertainty. He trained his revolver on O'Brien. 'My girls are staying right here.'

O'Brien nodded to Tate. 'Take them out,' he said.

Mallory started to speak again, but saw that the muzzle of O'Brien's rifle was now elevated toward his groin. 'Damn you!' he grated out.

'Come on, girls,' Tate urged them.

'Do something!' Big Betty yelled. 'Hey, Wilson!'

The two women were pushed and pulled to the entrance, then through it. At that moment Wilson appeared at the top of the stairs, rubbing sleep out of his eyes. He wasn't wearing his big Enfield. 'What is it?' Then he spotted O'Brien. 'What the hell?'

Mallory's gun was still in his hand. He saw that the rifle was on Rueda, but he still couldn't bring himself to fire on O'Brien. He holstered the gun. 'They took the girls,' he said at last.

'What!' Wilson exclaimed. His dark hair was partially in his face, and he had done up only a few of his shirt buttons. 'You let that happen?'

Mallory eyed him with a dour glance. 'Why don't you stop it?'

The several early drinkers in the room had all frozen in place as soon as the threesome walked in. Now, with Tate, Webster and the girls out on the street, one thin fellow got up and left quietly. Then, across the street at the hotel, the stagecoach dusted up to a stop.

'Why don't you all just stay put?' O'Brien suggested. 'In a couple minutes they'll be gone.'

Wilson had regained his composure. He pushed some hair off his forehead and leaned forward onto the balcony railing. 'If those girls are on that stage when it leaves, buffalo dung, you better be on it with them.'

'You sure that gun of yours can talk as loud as your mouth does?' O'Brien answered him.

Wilson scowled. 'Maybe you'd like to

wait down there till I go get it, and find out,' he said in a malevolent tone.

'Why don't you go do that?' O'Brien responded evenly.

At that moment they all heard the stage driver yell at his team, and the stage pulled away down the street. They listened as the sound faded and disappeared. A moment later Uriah Tate came back inside.

'Let's go, O'Brien. They're gone.'

O'Brien hesitated, looking up at Wilson. Mallory glanced up there too, and nodded his head.

'Everything all right in here?' Tate asked O'Brien, glancing up at Wilson.

'Just get out of here, Tate,' Mallory said heavily. 'And the next time you come in here packing iron, be prepared to use it.'

'No saloon or other place of business in Sulphur Creek is off limits to the law, Mallory. Don't forget that.'

'Don't forget what I said, Tate. Now take your hired gun with you and get out of my saloon.'

O'Brien was shaking his head. 'You got clabber for brains, Mallory. The only ones that can maybe benefit from all this still-neck horse pucky are these two boneheads you hired to do your fighting for you.'

Mallory wanted to argue with that but saw too much truth in it. 'Maybe you didn't hear me. Get to hell off my property.'

Tate snorted. 'Come on, O'Brien. Our work is finished here today.'

O'Brien nodded, then looked directly at Rueda, who still looked tense and ready for confrontation. 'Oh, yeah? I can hear a gun scraping holster leather at fifty yards in a blue norther. In case my back looks like a nice target for you.'

Then he turned his back on them and followed Tate out through the doorway. Nobody tried to stop them.

* * *

When Tate went to the Lost Dogie in early afternoon he learned that Rose

Nicely had already left town. Hank Logan had gone off somewhere, and they found out from the thin bartender.

'Ever since Logan started acting crazy yesterday, Rosie got scared of him,' the emaciated-looking barkeep told them. 'She left late yesterday in her own carriage. I think she was heading home to Missouri.'

'She's not coming back?' Tate asked him. He was leaning on the long bar, with O'Brien beside him. O'Brien had decided to go with him just about everywhere now, until this crisis resolved itself. If Tate were back-shot, he realized, that would leave Jock alone in the world.

'No, she's gone for good.'

'Why is she scared of Logan?' O'Brien wondered.

'Oh, he's been acting strange since he got that telegram yesterday. Mad at everybody. Hit Rosie and made a bruise on her cheek. Fired me and then rehired me. Strapped on an old Colt.'

O'Brien remembered that Logan was a cousin of the crooked marshal he had

had to kill up in Colorado. 'Do you know what was in the telegram?' he asked.

The thin man nodded. 'I saw it. He got word that a relative of his, a city marshal up in Colorado, was murdered recently. By some mountain man. The law thinks the cabin where it happened was being lived in by a trapper. There was a name mentioned. O'Brien, I think. Say, ain't that your name, mister?'

O'Brien and Tate exchanged a look. 'So that's how you met Logan's cousin,' Tate said.

'He tried to kill me and steal my hides,' O'Brien said quietly. He turned back to the barkeep. 'And you think that's why he's been acting crazy?'

Another nod. 'I heard him mumbling to himself. About his family. Expecting him to make that killing right.'

Tate looked over at O'Brien. 'He ain't got the guts to draw down on you. But I guess you got another reason to watch your back.'

O'Brien shook his head. 'The spring

thaws must've uncovered them bodies. If I ever get back up that way, I'll explain it all to them.'

'You won't have to,' the bartender said. 'The telegram said they figured it all out and knowed Logan was a crook.'

'I suppose our Logan didn't mind that,' Tate guessed.

'That family don't seem to have hog sense,' O'Brien offered.

'I'll tell him you was looking for him,' the barkeep said.

Tate and O'Brien returned to the jail. Tate felt relieved to have the saloon girls gone at last. Webster was asleep at Tate's desk when they arrived back there. He awoke in embarrassment.

'I was just resting my eyes, Uriah.'

'Any NPM people been in here?'

'No, it's been real quiet.'

Tate told him about Rose's departure, and Webster acted as if that resolved everything. 'Good. Now we can get back to our regular work, by Jesus!'

'I'm going over to the hostelry,' O'Brien told Tate. 'I might ride out to see how Jock is doing with that housecleaning.'

Tate smiled. 'He's a good kid. Tell him I'll be home for supper. I got some paperwork here.'

O'Brien hadn't seen the Appaloosa for a couple of days, and it guffered when it spotted him. He stroked its nose. 'I know. But we'll be back on the trail before you know it.'

The hostler came over to him. 'I been feeding him like royalty. You ready to settle up?'

'No, I'm just taking him out for the day. Get his saddlery over here and I'll get out of your way.'

'He's a beautiful animal,' the hostler said. 'I could get top price for him if you're of a mind to make some easy money.'

O'Brien shot a diamond-hard look at him. 'Just bring his saddle over here. And quit trying to figure out how to sell my stuff.'

The hostler shrugged. 'He's your mount.'

As O'Brien threw the saddle blanket on he patted the horse's flanks. 'Hell, you been eating better than me. You can use some exercise.'

It was a pleasant ride out to Tate's cabin. It felt good to be aboard the Appaloosa again, and O'Brien could hardly wait to return to the open trail. When he hitched the horse to a rail outside the cabin, he called in to Jock.

'Jock! Come on outside, kid!' He wanted to show Jock a Schofield .45 revolver he kept in a saddle wallet for emergencies, to see if the boy prefered it to the Dardick Tate had given him. When there was no response, he went on up to the door and swung it open.

Jock lay on the floor in a pool of his own blood.

O'Brien stood stunned for a half-moment, then jammed the Schofield into his belt and hurried over to Jock. He knelt over him, and cradled the boy's head in his arm.

'What the hell happened, kid! Can you talk?'

Jock's eyelids fluttered open, and he tried a smile when he saw O'Brien.

'I knew you'd come. I called you. In my head.'

O'Brien felt a tightness in his throat that he hadn't felt since he was a boy back in the Shenandoah when a younger sister had contracted diphtheria. He examined Jock up close and saw the hole in his lower chest. A pool of blood had leaked out of it.

'Sonofabitch,' O'Brien muttered.

'It was Logan,' Jock grated out.

'What the hell?'

'Said he expected you here. Probably thought to back-shoot you.' He coughed. 'Mentioned satisfying a debt.' His voice made a rattling sound.

'Yellow goddam snake,' O'Brien growled. He carefully picked Jock off the floor. 'Just rest easy, boy. We're going for help.'

Jock had driven Tate's old buckboard wagon to the cabin, and it sat out in back. O'Brien carried him out there and laid him gently on its bed, with a blanket under him. Then he got aboard and drove back into town.

Tate had mentioned that the town had a local doctor, and had pointed the house out to O'Brien in passing. O'Brien drove there quickly, with Jock looking dead in the back of the wagon. When he carried Jock into the house, and saw that the boy no longer responded to him, he had a sinking feeling in his chest. The doctor met them at the door.

'My God. Is that Jock Sumner?'

'Help him, Doc. He's shot bad. I don't know how long it was before I found him there. He's lost some blood.'

Jock was deposited on an examination table in a small back room of the doctor's house, and the doctor, a young, thin fellow, hovered over him. 'I'll be honest with you. It don't look good. But at least he's still breathing.' He put a stethoscope on Jock's chest, and nodded. 'Well. I'll have to dig that lead out of there. You can wait in my parlor if you wish. It will be a while.'

'Do your best on him, Doc,' O'Brien said quietly. 'I'm going down to the marshal's office to tell Uriah Tate.'

'Tell him it looks bad,' the doctor said somberly. His face was slightly flushed. 'But I'll do my best. Mr — ?'

'O'Brien. I'll be back soon as I can get here.'

The doctor was shaking his head. 'He's just barely holding on.'

O'Brien gave Jock a long last look, and disappeared throuh the doorway.

7

'What did you say?' Uriah Tate was frowning at O'Brien. His flaccid face turned pale.

'It's a chest shot,' O'Brien said. 'There was a lot of blood. God knows how long he was lying there before I found him.'

'Oh, my God!'

'I took him to your doctor. Is he any good?'

Tate nodded absently. He wiped a hand across his mouth, slowly. 'It was that sonofabitch Wilson. He threatened Jock, by God! I'm going to kill that bastard if I have to back-shoot him.'

'It wasn't Wilson,' O'Brien said. He was standing before Tate's desk, and now leaned against the wall behind him, feeling very tired suddenly. 'It was Logan. Jock told me.'

Tate finally rose from his chair, still in

shock. 'Logan? That must be some kind of mistake.'

O'Brien shook his head. 'Jock got the idea Logan went out there to bush-whack me. Maybe because of that no-good cousin of his I killed in Colorado. I can't figure nothing else. When Jock figured it all out, Logan decided to silence him.'

Tate settled a wide-brim hat on his head and checked the ammo in his Colt. 'I've got to go see him.'

'I'll drive you down there.'

Back at Dr Scott's office the doctor had just finished removing the bullet from Jock's chest. He pulled a surgical mask off and sat down with Tate and O'Brien to report to them. He looked very fatigued.

'Well, I dug the lead out. I almost lost him. He has a collapsed lung. He stopped breathing for a couple min-utes.'

'But he's OK now?' Tate asked nervously.

The doctor shook his head. 'I can't

186

honestly say that. It may take several days to tell.'

Tate looked like he might fall off his chair. Jock was his life now. The reason for driving down to the office in the morning.

'Jesus,' he muttered.

'I'll keep him right where he is for now. You can feel free to drop in as often as you like. But I suspect there'll be mighty little change in the next couple of days. Sorry, Uriah.'

The doctor left them alone then, and they sat there quietly.

'If that kid dies . . .' Tate mumbled.

'If I hadn't had that run-in with that bastard cousin of Logan,' O'Brien said bitterly, 'this wouldn't have happened.'

'That don't lay no blame at your door,' Tate said heavily. 'There's no figuring how things can come back to bite your butt sometimes. Jock understands things like that.'

O'Brien rose. 'I'm walking down to the Lost Dogie,' he said. His Winchester was still on his horse's irons out at

Tate's cabin. But he still had the Schofield .45 tucked in his belt, the gun he had been going to offer Jock. He disliked sidearms, but it would have to do.

Tate got up too. 'What's on your mind?'

'I think you know.'

Tate nodded. 'I'll just walk along.'

At that same moment, at the Prairie Schooner, Hank Logan had just entered the place from a rear door, and had found Mallory in his office. Mallory was at a long, littered desk, and R.C. Wilson occupied a straight chair in a corner. Logan came in breathless, and went and leaned on to Mallory's desk.

'I got to get out of town! The kid's alive!'

Mallory and Wilson stared at him. 'What?' Mallory said in puzzlement.

'I went crazy, I guess. Went out there to surprise the hunter and kill him. For my cousin, up north. I busted in and it was just the Sumner kid. O'Brien was supposed to be there, damn it. The kid figured out what I was up to, and would have blabbed. So I shot him and run.'

'You shot the Sumner kid?' Mallory said incredulouly. 'Have you gone nuts, Logan?'

Wilson shook his head. 'I don't believe it.'

'It all got out of control. If the kid told that wild man . . . But now he might be alive! Somebody saw O'Brien taking him to Doc Scott's place. He might've already told that hunter I went after him.'

Wilson let a grin move his hard face. 'You're a dimwit, Logan.'

'What the hell were you thinking?' Mallory frowned at him. 'I heard you been acting weird the last day or two.'

Logan sighed heavily, and collapsed onto a chair near the desk. 'It was supposed to be payback.'

'Would you at least try to make sense?' Mallory said impatiently.

Logan looked at the floor. 'I got a wire a few days ago. Turns out this

O'Brien murdered my cousin up in Colorado.'

'Well, well,' Wilson purred.

'I'll be damned,' Mallory added.

'They figured out somehow he was coming this way, and he might stop here. Some trapper up there heard that O'Brien knows the Sumner kid. There's a flyer out on him. My uncle sent the wire, and he made it clear that if O'Brien was here, I was supposed to avenge the family name.'

Wilson laughed gutturally. 'Ain't that a little optimistic?'

'I knew I couldn't face that animal down. But if I didn't do something, my uncle would send somebody after me. Anyway, if I caught him unarmed, I figured I'd have a good chance.'

'I doubt it,' Wilson said casually.

Logan gave him a slow look, and sighed heavily. 'My barkeep thought he saw the hunter ride out to the cabin. He must've been wrong. But I figured I could bust in on him out there, shoot him in the goddam back if I could. I panicked when the kid figured out I'd come for O'Brien. Hell, it wasn't my fault he was there, was it?'

'You soulless sonofabitch,' Mallory muttered. 'You're worse than Purcell.'

'I guess I went a little crazy. It all seems kind of bizarre now. But we all hated that kid, right? He was a goddam trouble-maker.'

'And now you've given them a reason to rile up those reformers to start a shooting war,' Mallory said. 'Before we can take down their protectors. Nice job, Hank.'

Logan leaned toward the desk. 'I'm expecting you to help me, Luke. That wild man will be coming for me. You have to hide me.'

Mallory shook his head. 'No, no. You're not making the Schooner a tinder-box with a very short fuse. You've already taken the offensive away from us and handed it to Tate. Look, you can use my hunting cabin. You've been there. It's just a few miles outside of town, and I don't think Tate would

191

remember it's out there.'

Logan nodded, relieved somewhat by that idea. 'Could you spare Rueda to ride out there with me? And stay a few days?'

'Are you kidding? I need all the guns I've got, right here at the Schooner. Take that sorrel out back, and ride on out there while you still can. I don't want you here when they come looking.'

Logan accepted that advice reluctantly. A few minutes later he was riding out.

★ ★ ★

O'Brien and Uriah Tate had located the bartender at the Lost Dogie, and had heard more details about the telegram from Colorado.

'He acted real scared when he read that wire,' the bartender told them. 'He must be terrified of that uncle. I guess they're kind of a wild family. But I don't know what that's got to do with young Jock Sumner.'

'Are you sure he ain't hiding here in the building somewhere?' Tate asked him slowly.

'Hell, I'd tell you if he was, Marshal. I don't stick my neck out for nobody. No, he ain't been back here at all since he left earlier.'

'Did he leave you any written directions?' Tate pursued.

'Nothing,' the barkeep replied.

'If he don't come back here, where would he go?' O'Brien said.

The other man shrugged. 'Maybe down to the Schooner. If he was running scared. I think you know he's in tight with Mallory, Marshal.'

'He won't be there,' O'Brien said. 'He knows that's the first place we'd look for him. Even though he sleeps here upstairs, does he own any other property around here?'

Tate intervened, and shook his head. 'He don't, O'Brien.'

'I think Mallory owns a cabin south of town,' the barkeep offered.

Tate nodded. 'Oh, yes. I forgot that. Whereabouts?'

'You go south on the main road. About five miles down, you turn off to the east on a small trail. That's what I heard, anyway. I never seen the place.'

O'Brien leaned over the bar. 'We never had this little talk. You understand me?'

The barkeep swallowed hard. 'Yes, sir. I got it.'

Out on the street a couple of minutes later, Tate turned to O'Brien. 'I guess we have to check out the Schooner first.'

'Hmm. I got a feeling about that cabin. Why don't you drive me out to your place so I can get the Appaloosa? I might just ride out to that cabin.'

'I'll go with you,' Tate said.

O'Brien shook his head. 'No. If anything was ever my business, Uriah, it's this. You stick close to your office with Webster till I get back. We'll make more plans then.'

'I don't like this, O'Brien. I'm the law

here. I have to arrest Logan for what he done. He has to stand trial for this.' His voice choked up.

'None of that will be necessary,' O'Brien said.

Tate eyed him narrowly.

'Don't get in my way on this,' O'Brien told him.

Tate sighed heavily, and nodded. He knew he couldn't stop the hunter if he tried. 'I understand.'

O'Brien retrieved the Appaloosa soon thereafter and checked the ammo in his Winchester rifle before he rode off, leaving Tate at his cabin. A short time later O'Brien turned off the main road south onto a narrow wagon trail, and slowed his mount's pace as he studied fresh tracks along the trail. They were the tracks of the sorrel mare Mallory had lent Logan at the Prairie Schooner.

About a mile east of the main road the tracks left the narrow trail and headed off south again. O'Brien nodded to himself. 'All right, you bastard.'

He rode along for another quarter-mile. When he topped a narrow ridge fringed with sapling cottonwoods the cabin came into sight, at the bottom of a slight grade. O'Brien could see the sorrel's tracks leading right to the cabin. The horse was apparently picketed at the rear of the place.

'Yeah. There you are,' O'Brien said in satisfaction.

In the next instant a rifle shot came from the cabin. The lead tore at O'Brien's rawhides under his right arm, missing a direct hit by inches but grazing his ribcage. The horse whinnied and reared slightly, then a second shot split the air. Instead of striking O'Brien in mid-chest, it smacked into the Appaloosa's high neck.

O'Brien dismounted and slid the Winchester from its scabbard. But by the time he had it in hand he saw Logan desperately run out of the cabin and to his horse out back. For a moment he was hidden from view by the cabin, and then he was mounted and riding off.

'Goddam it!' O'Brien muttered.

He threw the Winchester to the ground and went to the Appaloosa. He slid his Sharps .500 buffalo gun from its scabbard on the other flank of the horse, with its tripod. He slammed the tripod into place.

Logan was a hundred yards away, and moving fast, but on open ground. O'Brien fit the big gun to the tripod. It had started raining, and it got into his eyes. Logan was 300 yards away, and becoming a very small target.

O'Brien knelt behind the gun and tried to find Logan in his sights. He wiped rain from his eyes. In moments it would be too late. Logan would be gone, maybe forever.

Logan was 400 yards away. O'Brien aimed carefully and patiently, as he had done all those times on a buffalo hunt. Logan was 500 yards away, barely visible through the rain. A bobbing, erratic target. O'Brien waited another half-moment. Logan came clear in his sights, a tiny figure out there, over 500 yards distant.

O'Brien carefully squeezed the trigger, and the Sharps exploded loudly.

Five hundred and fifty yards away, Logan kept riding. Six hundred yards. At seven hundred, he slowly slid off his horse and hit the ground. His mount kept running until it was out of sight.

O'Brien rose slowly and shook rain off his Stetson. He walked over to the Appaloosa and examined its wound. 'Oh, hell. You ain't hurt bad. I don't want to hear no fuss about it.'

The stallion made a guffering in its throat.

'Yeah. You probably saved my neck. I reckon you won't let me forget that, either.'

He resituated the rifles on the saddlery and mounted up again. It took just a few minutes to ride out to where Logan had fallen.

Logan was lying face up on hard ground, a large exit wound in his low chest. He was already bleeding out. He was still alive, and saw O'Brien dismount and come to stand over him.

'I didn't have . . . anything against you . . . it was them. Up north. I had to do something.'

'So you tried to kill a boy,' O'Brien growled.

'Get me help. I'm done with Mallory. I swear it. I'll close the Dogie down.' In a choking, muffled tone, 'Let me live.'

'You'll be dead before I get back to the cabin,' O'Brien said. He was holding the Winchester; now he returned to his horse and slid it into its saddle scabbard. He touched the wound on the horse's throat.

Logan coughed up some blood. 'That was my Spencer carbine. Just bought it last week over at Bailey's. Shoots real good.' A small grin stretched his lips, followed by another cough. 'Well. I guess this is it then. Sorry about your horse.'

O'Brien climbed aboard. 'He's been hurt worse than that hunting shaggies.' He regarded Logan with studied disdain. 'When you get to whatever hell there is for yellow-bellied kid-shooters, remember who put you there.'

Logan's face was very pale. 'I told them . . . you were the one . . . they had to get rid of.'

'You was right,' O'Brien answered him.

Then he wheeled the Appaloosa around and headed back to town.

8

Luke Mallory paced the floor of his office at the rear of the Prairie Schooner, very agitated. He had just gotten word that someone had boarded up the Lost Dogie and posted a big CLOSED sign on its front doors.

R.C. Wilson leaned against a nearby wall; Pedro Rueda was seated on the end of Mallory's desk. They watched Mallory pace silently.

'Avery Hawkins was seen leaving the place just before day-break this morning,' Mallory was grumbling. It was the day after O'Brien's encounter with Hank Logan out at Mallory's cabin, but he knew nothing of what had occurred out there yet.

'You go soft on them, they get bold,' Wilson offered. 'They'll have the whole damn town out in front here, demanding closure. We should have met this with force sooner.'

Mallory went and sat at his desk, heavily. 'It's not Hawkins,' he said. 'He might be back in Kansas City without his only gun, St Clair, if it weren't for Uriah Tate being behind him. And that wild man in buckskins backing Tate.'

'I can take him out whenever you give me the word,' Wilson said casually. He removed the Enfield Mark II revolver from its well-oiled holster, and swung its cylinder out to check its cartridges. 'I can put three slugs in him before he can find the trigger on that rifle of his. It's really no problem.'

Mallory eyed his top gun doubtfully. 'That's what Rabbit thought.'

Rueda remembered that confrontation, and his failure to challenge O'Brien when he had a clear opportunity to do so. He looked away from Mallory.

'I'm not Rabbit Purcell,' Wilson said in an iron voice. 'And don't ever forget it, Mallory.'

Mallory noted the chilling look on Wilson's face, and his demeanor changed.

'No offense, Wilson. I know you're the best. Hell, you backed Billy Bonney down once. I'm just getting nerved up about this now. With that goddam Logan shooting the Sumner kid and then lighting out like a scared rabbit, it's no wonder Hawkins felt like he could get away with that last night.'

'They don't even know half that cantina is yours,' Rueda finally said, grinning slightly. '*Los locos!*'

Mallory cast a heavy frown his way. 'If you'd drawn down on that hunter when you could, we might not be having this conversation now.'

Rueda's swarthy face colored slightly. 'You were there. Why didn't you shoot him?'

'That's what I hired you for,' Mallory said caustically.

Rueda was about to respond when the heavy bartender came in from the bar room. 'Excuse me, boss. One of our customers wants to see you. He just come in. Says it might be important to you.'

Mallory sighed. 'All right. Send him in.'

A moment later a young ranch hand came in. He was a regular patron, and sympathetic to the saloon owners. He looked sweaty and disheveled. 'Mr Mallory.'

'What is it, Barnes?'

'I thought you ought to know. I rode past your old hunting cabin earlier today. Hank Logan is dead.'

A weighty silence fell over the room. Mallory leaned forward on his desk, and Wilson slid his Enfield carefully back into its holster.

'*Jesus y Maria!*' Rueda whispered.

'Dead?' Mallory said incredulously.

'Yes, sir. I found him a half-mile from the cabin. While I was out looking for quail. He's got a hole in his chest you could stuff your fist in.'

Mallory uttered an obscenity under his breath and looked over at Wilson. 'O'Brien.'

Wilson nodded. 'Of course. He was tight with the kid.'

They all sat there absorbing that for a moment, then Mallory spoke to the young man. 'Thanks, Barnes. Your drinks are on me the rest of the week.'

Barnes grinned. 'Yes, sir, Mr Mallory. Oh. I brought the body in. It already had blowflies in the eyes. It's at the undertaker's.'

When he was gone, Mallory slumped back on his chair.

'Hey, you own the Dogie!' Rueda exclaimed.

Neither of them even looked at him.

'Now it's a fight for survival,' Mallory said after a moment or two.

'It always was,' Wilson said. 'Ever since that hunter arrived.'

'I've been a goddam fool,' Mallory muttered.

'Yes. You have,' Wilson said. 'Tate would never have made that move against the girls without that hunter to back him. But now you understand. Take that buffalo man out, and the whole thing collapses like a house of cards. The law, the NPM. Everything.'

Mallory nodded. 'All right. It's our only option. Take him at your earliest chance. But don't make it look like murder. I have to live here afterwards.'

'I'll just call him out,' Wilson said easily. 'He's not the type to back away from a facedown. After that, we'll demand Tate's resignation, and your mayor will probably back us. We'll put our own man in. Then we'll send the NPM packing.'

Mallory sat there absorbing that for a moment. Wilson was turning out to be a dangerous man. A fast gun with big ideas.

'Yes, Wilson. I think you're right.'

Pedro Rueda rose off Mallory's desk. 'I should have killed him when he murdered Rabbit,' he said to Wilson. 'I feel like I cheated myself. *Dios mio*, you must let me have first chance at him!'

It didn't escape Mallory's attention that Rueda had addressed his plea to Wilson, and not himself.

Wilson was shaking his head. 'I told you. You're not up to the job.'

'I won't call him out. I'll do it my way. Nobody will know how it happened.'

'I'd rather it was an open showdown than a back-shooting,' Mallory said flatly.

'I won't make you look bad.' Rueda grinned. 'Just think, *señor*, what you would be thinking if you didn't have Wilson.'

Wilson liked that, and joined Rueda in the grin. 'Hell, give him a day or two,' he said. 'Either way, O'Brien is a dead man. Then this town belongs to us.'

Mallory regarded his two hired guns silently for a long moment, wondering what kind of alliance he had gotten himself into. He sighed heavily. 'Fine,' he said.

★　★　★

Over at Marshal Tate's office O'Brien had just returned from the hostelry to check on his Appaloosa. The hostler

207

had removed the bullet from the horse's neck late yesterday, on O'Brien's return from the shoot-out with Hank Logan, and the animal's wound was already healing. O'Brien took a big apple for a treat, and applied a poultice to the healing wound.

Now he washed up in a tin bowl back by the cells, while Tate sorted papers on his cluttered desk. O'Brien returned to the front of the place just as Tate was tacking up a Wanted dodger.

'I'm going over to see Jock,' he said as he approached. He was bare-headed and his wild, dark hair was slicked back. He had quit shaving and was growing a beard. He often did so out on the trail, and at times like this.

'I was there all the time you was gone yesterday. He just won't wake up. It don't look so good. I'm waiting for Webster; maybe he knows something.'

Tate started to say something else about Jock, when Webster walked in. Webster hadn't been told yet about Hank Logan.

'Oh, Webster,' Tate greeted him. 'Good. I want you to see these new posters.'

Webster glanced at O'Brien. 'I stopped past the doc's office. That kid ain't going to make it.'

O'Brien gave him a deep scowl. 'So you got that all figured out?'

'Hey, I'm just reporting facts.'

'You ought to learn to keep your mouth shut once in a while,' Tate told him. 'After you look at these posters, you can walk down to the undertaker's and deliver a paper to him on Hank Logan.'

'Hank Logan?'

Tate sighed. 'Yes, he's dead. O'Brien here shot him.'

O'Brien was situating his Stetson onto his head, and retrieving his rifle from where it leaned against the wall. Webster, looking frail and rather small next to O'Brien, squinted down on the hunter. 'You killed Hank Logan? Are you crazy!'

Tate walked over to him. 'Have you

forgot that Logan shot Jock, Webster?'

'That wasn't never proved in a court of law!' Webster argued. 'The kid could've made a mistake. You don't just go around shooting people like that. We got laws here. Why the hell ain't you under arrest?'

'Webster,' Tate said tiredly. 'If your brains was dyamite, you couldn't blow the top of your head off. Logan was a cold-blooded killer. He tried to kill O'Brien out there at the cabin.'

'Why do you bother?' O'Brien said, not even looking at Webster. 'I'll be back shortly, Uriah.'

'Watch your back out there,' Tate told him.

I kind of liked Logan, Webster said to himself.

Tate was shaking his head as O'Brien exited the office.

He arrived at Dr Scott's house a few minutes later. The doctor met him at the door.

'Any change, Doc?'

'I just took his temperature, and his

fever seems to be breaking. I was worried there for a while.'

'So that's good, ain't it?'

'It's very good. He said your name a couple of times, when the delirium was in him.'

'I'll be damned.'

'The wound is looking better now. I got a little soup down him earlier, but he didn't even know it was happening. He's quiet now, but you can go on in. Feel free to talk to him. It might help.'

O'Brien was led into the examination room, where they had situated Jock on a narrow bed in a far corner. 'Stay as long as you like.'

A moment later O'Brien was alone in the room with Jock, sitting on a straight chair beside the bed. He removed his Stetson and grimaced slightly. Under the rawhide tunic he wore a rib bandage from the confrontation with Jock's would-be killer.

He ran a thick hand through his hair. 'I got Logan, Jock.'

Jock lay there quietly, eyes closed.

'You're beating it, kid. You got a lot of your uncle in you. I knew you'd fight back.'

There was a low moan from Jock's throat.

'You get well, I'll take you out on a long hunt the next time I get through here. We'll stay out a month, let the trail provide for us.'

Jock's right hand moved. O'Brien hesitated, then took it in his. In another moment, the boy's eyes fluttered open. He focused on the hunter.

'O'Brien.'

O'Brien let a rare grin move his square, rugged face. 'Morning, kid.'

Jock tried to sit up, but was too weak.

'Just lay back there. You'll be up soon enough. Your wound is looking good.'

'Did I hear you say . . . you killed Logan?'

'He's lying down at the undertaker's with quarters on his eyes. If it was up to me, the turkey buzzards would be feeding on his ugly carcass now.'

Jock smiled. 'Everything my uncle

said about you is true.'

O'Brien sighed. 'Put all that stuff out of your head. You'll have your own stories to play out.' He noticed Jock's hand in his, and withdrew in embarrassment. 'I'm going to get the doc back in here. He might want to take your temperature again.'

Jock looked better with every moment. He watched the hunter rise from the chair. 'O'Brien.'

'Yes?'

'Thanks.'

'I owed you, kid. For bringing this Logan trouble down here with me.'

'That's on them Logans. Not you.'

'I'll just get the doc,' O'Brien said.

Later that day Jock took soup twice, and by the following morning he was asking for solid food, and sitting up to eat it. He told the doctor and anybody else who would listen that he had recovered so well because of O'Brien's presence, and his expectation that Jock would recover. O'Brien and Tate visited him together in the morning, and Tate was very emotional about Jock's recovery. The doctor said that Jock could be taken home that noon, but Tate decided to make up a soft bed for him at the jail, in a cell next to where O'Brien slept at night. Both men were afraid to leave Jock alone for any length of time at the cabin, and felt he could be watched over better at the jail.

Unknown to him, O'Brien's every move was being monitored by Pedro Rueda. O'Brien had walked down to the hostelry alone the night after Jock had woken, and Rueda had followed him down there, skulking in shadows. But he was very scared of the buffalo hunter, and wasn't satisfied that a good opportunity had presented itself to make an attempt on O'Brien's life.

At the Prairie Schooner, Wilson's patience was wearing thin. He figured he could end the drama at any moment he chose, and was sorry he had given Rueda a first chance at O'Brien.

'You've got another twenty-four hours,' Wilson told him on that second evening after Jock's waking. 'Then I'm doing it.'

In the meantime, Uriah Tate was playing nursemaid to Jock, with the doctor making daily calls. The morning after Wilson's ultimatum to Rueda, Jock got out of bed and came up front to the office, with Tate helping him walk. He was seated on a pillowed chair there, and had a cup of coffee with Tate and Webster. Tate was at his desk, with Jock close by. Webster sat on a straight chair in a corner, looking at a Kansas City newspaper. He could read just a little better than O'Brien.

'By God. They got electric lights in Boston now.'

'Yes, we all know that, Webster,' Tate said, looking up from his coffee cup. 'Are you comfortable, Jock?'

'I'm just fine, Uriah. Quit worrying over me.' They were changing a big bandage on his chest twice a day but he was gaining strength with every hour that passed.

'Yeah, I told him that,' Webster said.

Tate and Jock exchanged a look.

Webster had acted almost displeased when his prediction of Jock's demise proved to be wrong. Now that he associated Jock with O'Brien, his mild resentment of the boy had festered in him.

'Are things still quiet in Dodge City?' Jock asked him, to be pleasant.

'I never read about Dodge,' Webster said curtly. 'Say, that ain't my bed pillow you got behind you there, is it?'

'For God's sake, Webster. That's his own pillow. What if it was yours? You want him to get well, don't you?'

'It just looked like my pillow for a minute there.' The deputy looked quickly back down at the paper.

'Don't you have something to do back there?' Tate said irritably.

The front door swung open, and O'Brien came in, looking big and dangerous with the Winchester hanging from his right hand. He had taken a walk up Main Street to buy some extra ammo for his Sharps rifle. They all focused their attention on him as he leaned the rifle against a wall and poured himself a cup of coffee. Jock had smiled as soon as he saw him.

'Everything OK out there, O'Brien?'

O'Brien nodded. 'It seems awful quiet at the Schooner, though.' He stood there near the pot-belly stove, his presence filling the room.

'They're figuring out how to kill you.' Webster grinned.

Tate was furious. 'All right, that's it. Take a broom and go sweep up back by the cells. I'm tired of hearing from you this morning.'

'I swept up last night,' Webster protested.

'Then sweep up again,' Tate fairly yelled at him.

Webster threw the newspaper on to the chair he had occupied. 'You never treated me like this before *he* showed up here!' He jerked a thumb toward O'Brien.

O'Brien grabbed him by his vest, and dragged him toward the door. Webster's arms flailed wildly.

'Hey! What are you doing?' he yelled in a high, shrill voice.

O'Brien opened the door with his free hand, and spoke into Webster's face so close that it took Webster's breath away.

'Now you go take a walk. If you come back before noon, you'll deal with me.' Then he shoved Webster out onto the street.

Webster blustered out there, breathless. 'Uriah!'

O'Brien closed the door on him, and went back to the stove to retrieve his cup of coffee. Jock and Tate were both grinning widely.

'I wish I'd done that,' the marshal admitted.

'That man gets right in your craw,' O'Brien muttered, taking a sip of the hot coffee.

'Thanks, O'Brien.' Jock smiled.

'You're looking good today,' O'Brien told him.

'You know that Webster was right, don't you?' Jock said.

O'Brien regarded him with a slight frown. 'Don't give that a thought.'

Tate leaned forward on to his desk. 'Nobody has ever beat Wilson in a face-down. And I see Rueda as a back-shooter.'

'I know all that, Uriah.'

Tate sighed. 'You've already given us more than I could ever have expected. The prostitutes gone. The Dogie closed down. The NPM quieted down. Do me a personal favor now, O'Brien. Ride out before one of them murderers figures out a way to kill you.'

'I agree,' Jock said quietly, looking at the floor.

O'Brien set his cup down. 'Look. I kind of started something here. They might not be happy now just taking me out. Wilson took over a town out in the territories once, with a few cronies. I told you, I think he plans the same here. And you'd be in hs way. And there's Jock, if something happens to you. No. This town ain't safe now till all of Mallory's guns are gone. I have to

219

play this hand out.'

'I knew you wouldn't go,' Jock said in a half-whisper. He was sorry O'Brien was staying, but very relieved at the same time.

Tate glanced toward the front window. 'Oh-oh. We got company.'

In the next moment, Nell Douglas strode through the door, with NPM member Ned Tanner close behind her. Nell looked small standing there, with a shawl wrapped tightly around her shoulders and the habitual prayer book clasped in her hands. Tanner hung back behind her, and closed the door after them. Nell drew herself up to her full but slight height.

'Good morning, Marshal.'

Tate nodded, and set his coffee cup down. 'Nell. Tanner.'

Nell spotted Jock, and walked over to him. 'Oh, there you are, you poor child! Are you feeling well, Jock? Are you being treated well?'

Jock had always liked Nell. 'Everything is going great, Nell.' He remembered defending her at the Prairie Schooner that night, which seemed like a hundred years ago now. 'How are things at the NPM?'

'They will be better when all of this drinking and violence are a thing of the past in this town,' she responded. She looked over at O'Brien, who stood leaning against the wall now, and moved farther away from him with a scowl.

'What brings you here on such a quiet spring morning?' Tate asked her pleasantly.

'We're a delegation from NPM,' Nell declared, jutting her chin out.

'Oh. To thank us for getting the Lost Dogie closed, I suppose. And all the girls gone.'

Nell sighed. 'We understand this man here killed Hank Logan.'

Tate frowned. 'Yes, that's right. But it was in self-defense, Nell. And Logan tried to kill Jock. You must have heard.'

'Webster was down talking to us, saying there should have been a trial.

That sounds right to me, Marshal.' She shot a dark glance at O'Brien. 'We think there's been a lot of unnecessary violence since your friend here came to town. We wanted these saloons closed without that kind of trouble. We don't condone this kind of behavior, and never will. Blessed are the meek, Marshal, for they shall inherit the earth.'

'We would like O'Brien to leave Sulphur Creek,' Tanner blurted out, from behind her.

Jock was angry. 'Nell! What's the matter with you people! If it wasn't for O'Brien, this town would be at the mercy of killers!'

'But he himself is a killer,' Nell argued quietly.

'Maybe I better excuse myself,' O'Brien said.

'No, you stay put,' Tate said to him. 'Look, you two. You got no idea what's going on over there at the Schooner. Do any of you remember St Clair, for God's sake? There might be more of you over at Boot Hill if it wasn't for the law here. And O'Brien has been like having an unofficial deputy. You think any of them is scared of Webster? It's O'Brien that's standing between you and complete anarchy here.'

'Exactly!' Jock chimed in emotionally.

'I tried to get him to ride out,' Tate went on. 'But he ain't the kind of man to run from trouble. If you want to pray for deliverance, pray that he won't change his mind.'

Nell looked subdued. She turned her gaze on O'Brien. 'If we've judged you too harshly, we apologize. But we despise violence, Mr O'Brien.'

O'Brien sighed. 'Ma'am. I never started a fight in my life. But sometimes trouble comes looking for you, whether it's invited or not. In this case, I think you brought that trouble here with you, like an extra duffel. And people like the marshal here had to deal with it. Sorry if we ain't handling it quite like you would. But you got another remedy. You can all pack up your bags and go back to Kansas City or wherever you come from.'

'Well!' Nell sputtered.

'He's telling us to leave?' Tanner huffed.

Tate was smiling at O'Brien's summary. 'Now, now, Nell. Nobody's asking you to leave Sulphur Creek. I still think we can work this all out satisfactory to everyone involved. Once Mallory's guns are gone.'

'Well, then. Ask them to leave our city,' Nell suggested.

O'Brien shook his shaggy head. 'I'll be back at my cell cleaning the Winchester if anybody needs me.'

When he left the office it was as if five people had left the room. Nell found herself breathing a bit more easily. 'I'm afraid of him,' she said.

'So is Mallory,' Tate said pointedly.

'Well. I've said what I came to say. You know how NPM feels about all this. I hope you try to accommodate our wishes, Marshal.'

'Tell that to Luke Mallory,' Tate replied.

Webster didn't return to the marshal's office until well beyond the hour imposed on him by O'Brien. When he walked in Jock had gone back to his cot to rest. Tate was filing some papers in a cabinet, and O'Brien was a short distance away, examining shotguns in Tate's gun case. They both turned to Webster as he entered.

'Oh. I'm glad you're back,' Tate said, moving to his desk and taking a small pile of money from a drawer. He laid it on a corner of the desk. 'This is a week's separation pay, Webster. You're fired.'

Webster's jaw dropped. O'Brien turned toward Tate in surprise, as he had had no notice of such an action.

'Fired! Is this your notion of a joke, Uriah?'

'I never been more serious, Webster. You been about as much use to this office as if I hired one of Ben Stiller's cows. You're as clumsy with that gun as a hog on ice, and you ain't got the brains to come in out of the rain. No,

I'm better off without you.'

'Why, you can't do this! You need a deputy here! Didn't I help you get them girls on that stage?' He looked over at O'Brien. 'It's him, ain't it? You're going to hire him in my place!'

O'Brien allowed himself a slight smile at that, and Tate was shaking his head. 'Do you think I'd keep somebody on who's been going to the NPM and making trouble for us here? Where else have you been? Have you talked with Luke Mallory?'

'Hell, no!' Webster replied a bit too defensively.

'Go get your things and get out, Webster. Maybe you can get a job poking cows at one of the ranches. It ought to be comforting being surrounded by critters that might be more scatter-brained than you.'

Webster's face turned red. He grabbed the bills off the desk, and cast a mean look at O'Brien. 'I ain't got nothing back there I want. But I won't forget this, Uriah.'

'Maybe you better leave while you still can,' O'Brien said.

That brief remark made Webster breathe more shallowly. He acted as if he was going to respond, but then thought better of it. He turned and exited in a rush, slamming the door after him.

Tate shook his head. 'How did I put up with that all this time?'

'He might be dumb,' O'Brien offered. 'But he could make more trouble. That seems to be what he's best at.'

'I reckon I'll go see if Jock managed to sleep through that,' Tate said.

O'Brien had closed the gun case. 'I'm going to see if I got another apple for the Appaloosa.'

* * *

Later, that evening, Webster walked into the Prairie Schooner and looked around. He was not welcome there, and several patrons took notice of him with surprise. He walked over to the bar, where two cowpokes were drinking red-top rye. The heavy-set bartender eyed him warily.

'What the hell do you want, Webster? You trying to commit suicide?'

'I want to talk to Mallory.'

'You sure that's a good idea?'

'Goddam it, where is he?'

The bartender shrugged. 'It's your funeral. He's back in his office. With Wilson and the Mexican.'

Webster took in a deep breath. He had slicked his hair back, under his beat-up hat, and had found a shirt that was less wrinkled than usual. He went to the office door and knocked.

Inside, Mallory was seated at his long desk, his two hired guns occupying chairs near him. 'OK, come in,' Mallory called out. He had been telling Rueda that his time had expired for dealing personally with O'Brien, and that Wilson would be handling the job.

They all looked a bit incredulous when Webster walked in.

'Well, looky here,' Wilson grinned. 'A

ferret dressed up just like a man!'

'*Por Dios*!' Rueda exclaimed.

'What the hell do you think you're doing in here?' Mallory growled. 'Come to arrest somebody maybe?'

'I left Uriah Tate,' Webster said. 'I'm here as a friend.'

'We've got enough friends,' Wilson said drily.

Webster eyed him warily. 'I know you got reason not to believe me. But you might change your mind when you hear me out.'

'Why don't you go find a hole to crawl in?' Rueda suggested.

'You're telling us you quit Tate?' Mallory said.

'That's right. I had enough of that goddam buffalo man and the kid. I come to offer you information you might be able to use.'

'What could you tell us we don't already know?' Wilson said uncertainly.

Webster turned to him. 'You think I don't know you'd like to be rid of O'Brien? Well, I can help you with that.'

Mallory grunted out a small laugh. 'He must have really gotten under your skin, huh, Webster?'

'You don't know the half,' Webster said.

'What are you expecting for this information?'

'Nothing. Just knowing I helped take him down.'

'Well?' Mallory said. 'What do you have?'

Webster took another deep breath in. 'Don't never let this get back on me.'

'Get on with it, Webster.'

'Well. You all know he carries that Winchester with him wherever he goes. Even at the office it's always within easy reach. But he goes down to the hostler's regular to see to that horse of his. He treats it like it was a damn person. Anyway, when he's with the stallion, he puts that rifle aside and puts his attention on the animal. The hostler told me. He's defenseless then. And he'll be there tonight.'

A thick silence settled over them like

a night fog. Mallory and Wilson exchanged serious looks.

'*Caramba*,' Rueda murmured.

'Well. That might be helpful, Webster. You know, just to get him alone to warn him off. Nothing violent, of course.'

Webster smiled a thin smile. 'Of course.'

'We appreciate you bringing that in here,' Mallory added. 'Go tell the barman you can take a bottle of planter's rye home with you.'

Webster's smile widened. 'Much obliged, Mallory.'

'And if you ever need some odd-job work, feel free to come to me first.'

'That's real good of you,' Webster said. 'Well. You boys have yourselves a nice evening.'

When he had gone Mallory turned to Wilson. 'This might be good. Our best chance of ending this quickly.'

'It is *perfecto*!' Rueda blurted out. '*Por favor*, let me have this last chance at him! I promise you. It will be finished this night.'

Mallory looked over at Wilson for his reaction.

'I'm not afraid of the hunter's rifle. I can take him any time you give me the go-ahead.' He was in one of his moods to let Mallory think he was still in charge. 'I have no objection to you getting your last chance at him, Pedro. We'll have a party here later. To celebrate taking control of this town.'

'I won't fail you,' Rueda said slowly. His breath was coming more shallowly, and he felt a new, paper-dry taste in his mouth. 'The hunter will not live to midnight.'

★　★　★

Uriah Tate fried eggs for them at the jail in late afternoon, and afterwards O'Brien joined Jock at Jock's cell before walking down to the hostelry. If Jock stayed up for more than a few hours he still got very tired. He had gone to his cot to have a rest before joining Tate and O'Brien again in mid-evening to discuss Mallory and his hired guns. Tate was doing some paperwork at his desk.

O'Brien went and sat on the foot of Jock's cot, propping the Winchester between his legs. 'I'm heading down the street to give that horse this last apple,' O'Brien said. 'I spoiled him rotten since he took that bullet for me. He'll be hard as hell to ride with now.'

Jock grinned at that summary. 'He's a beautiful animal. Uncle Wesley told me about him. He also said your parents were emigrants.'

O'Brien nodded. 'My daddy liked the Shenandoah because it reminded him of the Highlands back home. He was running from something back there. The toughest man I've ever known.'

'I wish I could have met him,' Jock said.

'You wouldn't have liked him. He could be an ornery sonofabitch. He was going to shoot our dog once because it got sick. But I stood between him and the dog with an eight-gauge and said if he shot the dog I'd shoot him. He walked away, and the dog got well. He said later that was the day he knew I was a man. I wouldn't've shot him, of course. But he always thought I would.'

Jock grinned. 'I like that story.'

'The only other person I told that to was your uncle,' O'Brien added.

Jock felt very close to him at that moment. 'O'Brien. When you ride south, I'd like to ride with you.'

O'Brien frowned heavily at him. 'Oh, hell, Jock.'

'I'd like the life on the trail. Hunting and trapping. Eating meals over a campfire. Breathing fresh air. I wouldn't be any trouble. I'd do the cooking.'

O'Brien shook his head. 'In the first place, it will be six months till you can ride the trail. And most important, I'm a loner, kid. Oh, I take on a partner now and again. But I go my own way and do my own thing. It's always been that way. Anyway, you can't leave Uriah. You're his whole life now. We couldn't do that to him.'

Jock looked away, and gave a heavy

sigh. 'I guess you're right.'

'You know I am.' He rose with the rifle.

Jock looked up at him. 'I want you to live long enough to ride out.'

O'Brien frowned again, then grinned through it. 'Get some rest, Jock.'

Less than a half-hour later O'Brien was on his way to the stables. It was still early evening, and the sun was still up in the western sky. O'Brien was becoming over-satiated with town life and hungry for the trail. If it weren't for Jock, he would have been gone by now. But he felt it was even more important now for him to see this little 'war' through to its conclusion. Unlike in Dodge City a short time ago, when Wyatt Earp rode in to restore order, this fight had to play itself out without the intervention of big-reputation peace-keepers. In Sulphur Creek, it looked as if it had to be him, O'Brien, who had to see it through to the end.

'Your mount is doing just fine,' the hostler greeted him on his arrival at the stables. 'I was just about to take that last poultice off his neck.'

'I'll do that,' O'Brien told him. His beard was getting thicker, which gave him an even more primitive look. 'He'll expect it. He thinks he's the Prince of Arabia right now.' He laid his Winchester aside.

'You got a beautiful animal there,' the hostler offered.

'Don't tell him. His head is puffed way up already.'

'Well. Take your time with him. I'll be out back unbaling some hay.'

The stallion guffered when it saw O'Brien, and nuzzled him with its nose.

'All right, all right,' murmured O'Brien, 'let me get that poultice off you.'

He took the bandage off the horse's neck; it was smeared with medicine, wet drainage and a small amount of blood. But the wound was just about healed.

'Well, by Jesus. You been putting one over on me. You're good as a gold piece.'

The horse guffered again as O'Brien took the poultice to the big open doorway to discard it in a trash container.

When he arrived there, Pedro Rueda stepped out from the building corner and aimed his Joslyn .44 at O'Brien's heart.

'*Buenas noches*, hunter,' he said with a dark grin.

They were almost nose to nose. O'Brien glanced toward his rifle, but it was twenty feet away.

'No, no. It is much too far,' Rueda cooed. 'You have made a big mistake, Señor O'Brien. Your great reputation will not help you now.'

'Evening, Rueda,' O'Brien said casually. 'You here to steal saddles?'

Rueda's face went somber. 'You remember that day at the Schooner? When you made me back down after you murdered Purcell?'

'I thought you acted with more sense than I give you.'

Rueda snorted his contempt. But his

cheeks were flushed, and when he spoke, it was breathlessly. 'You embarrassed me there. I listened to my head. About the stories I heard. But look at you now. Where are the stories now, Mr hunter? Where is your *calidad de invencibilidad?*'

'You're the one making a mistake, Rueda. Put that thing away and ride out, and you'll live through this. You're just a pawn for Wilson.'

Rueda was red-faced. 'I will live through this? I am a pawn? Your big talk will not save you, hunter! You're caught naked, get it? *Adios*, and say *hola* to Rabbit for me!'

He aimed the revolver at O'Brien's mid-chest and his finger tightened over its trigger, but in that half-second O'Brien hurled the poultice into Rueda's smug face.

The smelly bandage landed flat against Rueda's nose and mouth, and partially blinded one eye for an instant. In that instant, O'Brien grabbed at Rueda's gun hand and shoved it away just as it fired. The explosion made O'Brien's left ear ring as the lead whistled past his head and tore up a rafter in the overhead timbers. As O'Brien's iron grip closed on the gun hand, bones audibly snapped in it, and another wild shot rang out, simultaneous with Rueda's piercing scream. Rueda tried to throw a punch into O'Brien's jaw, and the blow glanced off as O'Brien wrested the Joslyn from his grasp. With his free hand he slammed Rueda against a thick door jamb, cracking a rib in his back. Then the muzzle of the gun was pressed against the Mexican's forehead. O'Brien's finger closed down over the trigger.

'*Dios mio! Por favor!* Do not shoot me!'

'Why not?' O'Brien growled into his face.

Rueda was holding his crushed hand to his chest, and squinting in pain from that and the fractured rib. 'I will do what you ask. Just don't kill me,' he gasped out breathlessly.

O'Brien hesitated. Then, 'Ride out of here, Mex. And don't never come back.'

Rueda nodded vigorously through his pain and fear. '*Sí*. Yes!'

O'Brien dropped the revolver to his side, and Rueda hesitated for just a moment, to make sure he had permission. Then he turned and ran to a horse tethered to a post outside the door. He climbed awkwardly aboard just as the hostler walked up behind O'Brien. Then Rueda was spurring the mount away without looking back, heading out of town.

'Hey! That's my horse!' the hostler yelled, waving his arm around. He watched Rueda disappear past some buildings. 'Sonofabitch!'

'Stupid damn Mexican,' O'Brien grumbled. He turned the Joslyn .44 over in his hand. 'Nice balance. Here. You take it. It's worth more than that mangy mare of yours.'

The hostler took the gun and looked it over. 'Well. Thanks.'

'He won't be back for it,' O'Brien said.

'I saw what you done. He had this thing aimed at your heart. How did you do that?'

O'Brien turned an impatient look on him. 'You got any carrots back there somewhere?'

The other man stared at him. 'Carrots?'

'Yeah. Carrots. The Appaloosa asked for one. Don't worry. I know that will be extra.'

The hostler was still trying to understand all that had happened. 'Carrots. Sure, I got carrots.' He looked off in the direction Rueda had ridden. 'I don't know how you done that.'

'And make sure his hay is dry,' O'Brien added. Then he walked over to his horse with the hostler still staring after him.

9

When O'Brien returned to the jail and reported his encounter with Rueda, Uriah Tate and Jock were very pleased, but had mixed feelings about the whole thing.

'He just rode out?' Jock said.

'I gave him a little nudge.' O'Brien grinned slightly at him.

'My head is spinning,' Tate admitted. 'So he went down there to kill you?'

'That was the idea I got,' O'Brien told him. He laid his rifle against the nearby wall. 'Sent by Mallory, I reckon. Him and Wilson letting the Mex do their dirty work.'

'Will he come back?' Tate wondered.

O'Brien cast a slow look on him. 'I'd be surprised,' he suggested. He went and poured himself a cup of coffee at the stove, then leaned against the wall. 'The stallion is healing real good. He's ready to ride when I am.'

Jock and Tate exchanged a smile. But then Jock's face went sober. 'They decided to come after you. And now it will be Wilson.'

'That's right,' Tate agreed, in a hushed tone. 'Now it will be Wilson.'

'They'll come after both of us,' O'Brien said, leaning against the wall.

Tate nodded. 'I know.'

'Then you'll stand together against them,' Jock said, his cheeks flushed. 'You're the only ones between this town and Wilson.'

O'Brien smiled at him. 'Don't fret it, kid. Everything will be fine.'

Tate sighed. 'You've been a godsend for us here, O'Brien. But now we have Wilson. He can draw that Enfield so fast you can't see it clear leather. And he hits what he aims at. He's killed a few lawmen and gunslingers already. Without raising a sweat. He'll be gunning for you.'

'Then I'll have to kill him, won't I?'

Jock and Tate just sat there staring at him silently.

'What's our next move then?' Tate said at last.

'We won't have to make a move,' O'Brien told him. 'They'll call us out.' He folded his arms across his chest. The wound he had received from Logan was almost healed under his rawhides. 'We stay put here till then. You got a little grub stored up in the back, Uriah. No need exposing ourselves to ambush out there, and leaving Jock undefended.'

Jock was surprised by the take-charge manner O'Brien displayed when the circumstances demanded it. 'Don't give me a second thought,' he said. 'I still have the Dardick Uriah gave me.'

'For God's sake, boy!' Tate protested. 'You have trouble getting off your cot.'

O'Brien grinned slightly at the exchange. 'Better lock that front door. I'm going to go wash up.'

About an hour later, over at the Prairie Schooner, the hostler came into the saloon for a drink and reported to Mallory that Rueda had ridden out.

Mallory was arranging bottles on a shelf with his barman, and was so shocked he had to go lean on the bar for a long moment.

'I don't believe it,' he muttered to himself. 'This is getting to be goddam ridiculous.'

The hostler had already ordered his drink at the bar when Mallory walked over to a table where Wilson was drinking alone. A couple of patrons noted Mallory's somber look as he passed.

'Rueda is gone,' he said heavily, sitting down with Wilson.

Wilson set his drink down, and leaned toward Mallory. 'Gone?'

'The hunter busted him up some. Took his gun. The hostler said he rode off like the Devil himself was after him.' He shook his head. 'I don't mind admitting it. I'm scared. There used to be six of us. Now there's just you and me.'

Wilson frowned at him. 'I knew you didn't have the stomach for this.'

Mallory looked down. 'Think what you want. The hostler says that wild man wasn't even armed. This is getting serious. Maybe I'll just make a deal of some kind with the NPM.'

'Or better yet, why don't we just put our tails between our legs and run? Let the crazies burn your place down. Is that what you want?'

Mallory got hold of himself. 'Of course not. But now it's us or him.'

'It's always been us or him. I'm not Rueda, Luke. I told you, I can take O'Brien. But this time we'll do it right. We'll kill them both.'

'Do you think we can really do that?'

'Hell, yes. We'll call them out. O'Brien would never back away from that. Tate will stand up with him, of course. I could probably handle that myself. But I wouldn't want any last-minute accidents. You'll be there, too. You handle a gun pretty well.'

Mallory stared past him, and took a deep breath. He took his Smith & Wesson from its holster on his hip, where he always carried it, and swung its cylinder out. 'I can hit a target when I have to.'

'It's your whole damn future in this town that's at stake,' Wilson told him.

Mallory looked over at him. 'If we pull this off, I'll make you a full partner, Wilson. That would be in the Schooner and the Dogie.'

Wilson grinned. 'If we pull this off, I'll own this town.'

Mallory studied Wilson's cold gray eyes in that lean, hard face, and knew that if they succeeded he would end up only with what Wilson gave him. A brief thought flitted through his head of making a deal with Tate. But he knew Wilson would never let that happen.

'That would be great,' he finally managed. 'But listen. Logan's bartender Jennings owes me, and he's good with a gun. I'm letting him stay above the Dogie rent-free. He'll stand up with us in a showdown.'

Wilson narrowed the hard eyes on him. 'Are you up to this, Mallory?'

Mallory shrugged. 'Is there anything wrong in raising the odds in our favor?'

'I don't need odds. But bring him in if you like.' He sat back on his chair, feeling very much in charge. 'I'm kind of warming to this now. When this is all finished, we'll make this town over any way we want. Pin Tate's badge on your friend Jennings. Maybe make your man the by-God mayor.' A short laugh. 'Hell, we can collect taxes. Bring in gamblers to make us quick cash. Don't worry, I'll make a place for you here. I'll make this saloon show a profit you never dreamed of.'

Mallory swallowed hard. 'I'm sure you would.'

Wilson looked very pleased with himself. 'Yeah. Jennings isn't a bad idea. All three of us will be out there. That way, I won't have any unpleasant surprises.' He grinned. 'I got too much to lose.'

'When should we do it?'

'As soon as you get your commitment from Jennings. Tomorrow. The next day. I want to make some plans. For afterwards.'

'We can have privacy in my office,' Mallory said hopefully.

'You just get Jennings,' Wilson told him. Then he rose, walked over to the bar by himself and ordered a London gin.

It was obvious he didn't want company.

$$\star \quad \star \quad \star$$

Over at the Frontier Hotel, where Avery Hawkins had taken a room, Nell Douglas and Ned Tanner had arrived to discuss the present situation with him. Nell insisted on beginning their informal meeting with a reading from a book of scripture she had brought with her.

''He who practices sin originates with the Devil, because the Devil has been sinning from when time began. So down the great dragon was hurled, the original serpent, the one called Devil and Satan, who is misleading the entire

249

inhabited Earth.'' She closed her eyes and lifted her face upward. 'Lead us through this valley of death, all-knowing God, and deliver us from this evil. Amen.'

'Amen,' Hawkins and Tanner echoed impatiently.

'As I said when I came in,' Nell then went on. 'Another violent killing was narrowly avoided at our hostelry just today, and it involved that man O'Brien again. It's time you did something, Avery.'

'That's right.' Tanner nodded. 'I understand he crippled the Mexican.' Tanner never had an original thought of his own, and had recently been adopting all of Nell's positions as his own.

Avery Hawkins, though, had been taking much notice of the way things were developing. 'You two do understand that Rueda was about to kill O'Brien?' he said with a frown.

'He draws violence to him like the cholera to an Indian,' Tanner said rather loudly.

Tanner and Nell were seated on a short sofa across the room from Hawkins's bed, and he had drawn up a straight chair facing them. He clasped his hands before him and spoke as he stared down at them. 'A few days ago we were worried about the hired guns at the Schooner and the Dogie. Now three of those gunmen are gone, one way or another. The saloons are safer places now. One is even closed down. All because of the hunter.'

'Then you condone killing as a means to our end?' Nell said flatly.

'You know better than that, Nell. But O'Brien hasn't murdered anyone. He's just responded to threats and violence on the part of the saloon people. Uriah Tate would have arrested him if he had cause.'

'Would he?' Nell said. 'I get the idea they're friends now.'

'They're thick as thieves!' Tanner cried out.

'Well. Everything they've done has worked out to our advantage,' Hawkins said. 'The prostitutes are gone. Before the hunter arrived here, that was going nowhere. The Lost Dogie is closed, maybe for good. We're getting everything we came here for.'

'But at what price?' Nell said.

Hawkins met her gaze. 'Let's try to remember who started all of this. Just like O'Brien reminded us. We did. Now that it's spiralled out of our control, we're indignant. I have to tell you, I doubt that any of the good things would have happened without that buffalo hunter. We have to accept the consequences of our crusade here. Or go try it somewhere else.'

'Maybe that's not such a bad idea,' Nell said heavily. Her small, buxom figure had slumped into itself. 'So the killings will stop.'

Hawkins stared at her, realizing the depth of her lack of understanding. 'Nell, Ned, I don't think you get the current situation here in Sulphur Creek.'

Nell looked up at him.

'It's gone way beyond this little spat with the NPM, for Mallory and his hired killer Wilson. Mallory obviously sent Rueda to the hostelry to kill O'Brien. In doing that, he stepped over a line. The marshal would be honor-bound to arrest all of them if that had succeeded, and they would never allow that to happen. So the marshal would have to be killed too. Don't you see? Then the town would belong to them. They would run us out on a rail if they wanted to. The NPM would be dead in Sulphur Creek. The town itself would be dead.'

'Dear Jesus in heaven,' Nell whispered. 'What have we wrought here?'

'Our motives were good,' Hawkins said.

'Everything bad in this is on the hunter,' Tanner said stubbornly. 'We could have done all this peaceably.'

'That doesn't seem likely,' Hawkins said.

'No,' Nell conceded. 'It doesn't. What do we do now, Avery?'

Hawkins blew his cheeks out. 'I don't know. One thing seems fairly certain. There's going to be a monumental struggle between the law here and Luke Mallory, and that struggle is imminent. If Mallory and Wilson win, we might as well pack our bags. Sulphur Creek will be too dangerous a place for the NPM. And for you, Nell.'

'I don't back away from a fight against evil!' she said firmly. 'The Lord will protect me from Mallory's iniquitous ways. An angel came to me, and said, 'Have no fear, Nell, for you have found favor with God.''

'Amen,' Tanner barked.

'I want you to know in advance, Nell. If I can help Uriah Tate in any way, I will. Even if that means being in league with the hunter.'

Nell sighed. 'I'll pray for you, Avery.'

'That will be appreciated, Nell.'

The next morning came peacefully to Sulphur Creek. Word had spread around town that a showdown appeared to be brewing between Marshal Tate and Luke

Mallory, and that that meant a confrontation between Wilson and the stranger in town who wore buckskins and called himself O'Brien.

All day that day after Rueda's precipitous flight from town, citizens stayed at home and indoors. The streets of the city were deserted. Even nearby ranchers had heard of the impending eruption of violence, and had kept their cowhands out of town.

Luke Mallory walked down to the Lost Dogie at mid-morning, pried a board off the front entrance, and woke up the barkeep Jennings, who was still in bed in an upstairs room. He came down the staircase in yellowing long underwear and wrinkled trousers.

'Oh. Mr Mallory. I was just getting up.'

'Yeah. Come on down here, Jennings, I want to talk with you.'

Jennings came and leaned against the long bar with Mallory. The Dogie wasn't quite as plush as the Schooner, but there was a Remington painting behind the bar, depicting Sioux Indians on the warpath.

'I've decided to put you back on salary, Jennings,' Mallory began. 'I'll be reopening the Dogie any day now.'

A grin spread across Jennings's thin face. 'Yes, sir. And much obliged. I been kind of keeping guard here for you.'

Mallory grunted. 'I guess I'll be seeing you at Hank Logan's funeral in a couple of days?'

'Oh yes, sir. Mr Logan was a good boss.'

'What do you think of that O'Brien murdering him out there at the cabin?'

Jennings formed a mild scowl. 'Why, I hope that bastard fries in hell!'

Mallory nodded with a small smile. He noted that Jennings had strapped on a Wells Fargo revolver similar to the one Maynard McComb had worn. 'I see you're carrying.'

Jennings grinned. 'Like I said. I've been sort of watch-dogging it over here. There's a lot of valuable stuff in here. Not counting the inventory.'

'Logan told me you're pretty good with that thing.'

'Oh, I entertain myself with it quite a bit. I used to shoot targets in a medicine show. Of course, I'm a little rusty now.'

Mallory's smile had widened. 'That's just great, Jennings. The medicine show thing. Maybe you can still do something for Hank besides showing up at his funeral.'

'Oh. Really?'

'We're going to stop the killings. Wilson and me. And avenge Hank Logan's and Rabbit Purcell's murders. And we want you with us.'

Jennings was frowning. 'How do you mean, Mr Mallory?'

'We're calling them out. The marshal and that murdering buffalo hunter. I want you to stand with us.'

Jennings ran a hand across his mouth. 'You mean, a facedown.'

'That's right.'

'And that O'Brien will be there.'

'That's what we're counting on.'

'Well, the thing is, you see, all I ever shot at was targets, Mr Mallory. I never shot a man in my life.'

'If you can hit targets, you can hit a man.'

'Except the targets don't shoot back.'

Now it was Mallory who was frowning. 'I never figured you as yellow, Jennings. Was I wrong?'

'Uh. No, sir. It's just I never done nothing like this before. Say, what about your own barkeep? Suggs, ain't it? He might be more dependable in something like this.'

'He's never worn a gun in his life,' Mallory said flatly. 'No, it's you who has to help, Jennings. And I'm counting on you.'

'Well, I just don't know.' The fact was, the very thought of going up against O'Brien made his heart pummel at his chest and his stomach tighten.

'Hmmph. Well, let me put it this way. You help us in this, you're one of us. You don't, you're not. I couldn't even guarantee you'd have a job here at the

Dogie. Or anywhere else in town.'

Jennings looked quickly up at him. 'Oh, I didn't mean I wouldn't do it,' he said in an apologetic tone. 'I mean, I'll do whatever you ask, Mr Mallory. After all, we're all in this together, aren't we?'

'Exactly,' Mallory said with some acidity.

'When will this happen?'

'Probably in the next twenty-four hours. When you get dressed and cleaned up, come on down to the Schooner. You'll be staying there till this is over.' He turned to leave. 'And make sure that Wells Fargo is oiled and loaded.'

Jennings nodded rather glumly. 'I'll be down there in less than an hour.'

★   ★   ★

About thirty miles south and west of Sulphur Creek, in a tiny village called Bigosville, Pedro Rueda walked into the only saloon in town with a sullen look on his swarthy face. His right hand was bandaged and in a sling, and he walked with a limp, all because of his brief encounter with O'Brien. He stopped inside the doors and looked around. This was not the Prairie Schooner. The oak bar was a short one, with a greasy-looking bartender swatting at flies behind it. The floor was covered in sawdust, and the place smelled rankly of beer and urine. It was a warm day outside, and the thick air in the bar was almost unbreathable. There were two cowpokes sitting at a table close to the front doors, and a lone drinker at the rear, in shadow back there. Rueda made a sound in his throat and walked over to the bar.

'Afternoon, stranger,' the obese barkeep greeted him. 'New in town, are you?'

The Mexican hurled a deep scowl his way. 'Planters rye, and leave the bottle.'

'We don't have the Planters. We just got some nice rum in.'

'*Madre de Dios!*' Rueda grumbled. '*Sí*. OK. The rum.'

As he swigged the first drink down a moment later, he heard his name called out from the table at the rear. 'Hey! Rueda!'

He squinted down on the table in shadow, then finally recognized Maynard McComb, the hired gun of Hank Logan who had left town rather than continue on in the so-called Peace Commission formed by Mallory and Logan. Rueda picked up his bottle with his good left hand, and limped back to McComb's table.

'*Jesus y Maria*!' Rueda exclaimed as he seated himself beside McComb. 'What are you doing here, *compadre*? I thought you were in the Territory!'

'I've got a relative near here,' McComb told him. His husky frame hunched over the table, and his red hair stuck out on all sides of a narrow-brim hat. 'Why aren't you putting down Luke's best booze back at the Schooner?' He glanced at Rueda's hand.

Rueda shook his head, and ran his unbandaged hand through his thick, black mustache. 'I am finished with all of that. I should have left when you did.'

'What happened to your hand?'

Rueda gave him a dark look. 'That *diablo* of a man. The hunter. He is like a wild animal! They sent me to kill him. This is what happened.'

McComb grunted out a small laugh. 'I guess the stories were true.'

'I wanted no more of it. If they want him dead, let them kill him. I do not think it's possible.'

'Hmm,' McComb said, shaking his head and looking at the floor, trying to imagine that confrontation.

'He has killed two of us. But if anybody can take him on, it's Wilson. I wish him luck.'

'Wait a minute. He killed two, you said?' He had left town after Rabbit Purcell's demise at O'Brien's hands.

'You did not know? Yes, your boss is dead. The hunter killed him.'

McComb sat back on his chair and his face sagged into straight lines. 'I'll be a spine-back horny toad!'

'We think he killed Hank with that long gun of his. The buffalo gun. Blew a hole in him you could see through, *por Dios*!'

'That sonofabitch,' McComb said under his breath.

'*Exacto*. But we are well out of it now, *sí*?' He poured himself and McComb a shot glass of rum. 'Drink up, *amigo*. We celebrate our good sense. Let Wilson and Mallory handle it. They have the ambition. Not the likes of us.'

McComb was somber-visaged now. 'By Jesus. I ran out on Hank and let that buffalo man murder him.'

'He took a shot at the Sumner kid,' Rueda said. 'He went loco. You owe him nothing.'

McComb shook his head. 'That was stupid. Hank always was a little crazy. But I owe him, Rueda. He did me some big favors.'

'Oh, well. What is past is past, no? You and me, we are *afortunado*. To be out of it.'

McComb sighed heavily. 'You don't understand. I have to go back.'

Rueda got an incredulous look on his square face. '*Como?*'

'If Mallory is going against them, I should be there. For Hank.'

Rueda's sudden anger surprised even him. 'Hank Logan is dead. You cannot owe a dead man.'

'Yes, you can,' McComb told him. 'Me and Hank go back a long way. I told him I wanted no part of that Peace Commission. But now I see he was right. If that O'Brien ain't stopped, they might as well give the town over to the NPM. And that would be the end of things as we've always known them. Dodge City is teetering on the edge right now. Maybe this is where we should make a stand.'

Rueda was shaking his head. 'Wilson is not trying to stop a reform movement, *amigo*. He just wants the town for himself.'

'I don't care what Wilson wants,' McComb said. 'Men like him come and go. But once the saloons are gone, they won't come back. A man will be fined for spitting in the street. Sulphur Creek will be like Boston. The dirt farmers brought in by reformers have scared most of the wild game off, too. This is what Hank was against. I have to go back.'

'You are a fool!' Rueda told him. 'They intend to kill the marshal, too, you know.'

McComb looked past him. 'If Tate wants to put the NPM in power, then he's part of the problem.'

Rueda punched a cork into the top of his liquor bottle and rose from his seat. 'Well, if you ride back there tonight, you will probably be in time for it. *Buena suerte, mi amigo!* I believe you will need it. I am riding south as far and fast as my mount will carry me. I expect to be in Mexico tomorrow.' He gave a big grin. 'I will be thinking of you.'

McComb held his liquor glass up. 'I'll see you in hell, Rueda.'

Rueda nodded, wondering why this

gunman had any interest in the future of Sulphur Creek, or the honor of a man like Hank Logan. But the strangeness and unpredictability of his world never failed to amaze him.

'*Con mucho gusto*, McComb,' he responded. 'That will give me much pleasure.'

By late evening that day, the evening before Wilson's planned shoot-out, McComb was back in Sulphur Creek.

10

It was mid-evening when Maynard McComb strode unexpectedly into the Prairie Schooner and found Luke Mallory sitting with Wilson and Jennings at a table near the back of a rather quiet bar room. No locals were patronizing the saloon now, and just a few cowboys had ridden in, off the cow trail and innocent of what was brewing. The three at the table looked up at McComb quizzically.

'Well, I'll be damned,' Wilson muttered.

'Maynard!' Jennings exclaimed. He and McComb had become rather friendly at the Lost Dogie. 'What the hell!'

Mallory frowned hard at him. 'Good God, McComb. I thought you'd be off to California or someplace by now.'

'I never got farther than Biggsville,'

McComb said, casting a sober look at Wilson. 'I met Rueda there.'

'That little weasel,' Wilson offered.

'Sit down, McComb,' Mallory told him. 'Have a drink with us.'

McComb joined them, and poured himself a drink from a tall bottle.

'What are you back here for?' Mallory asked him after a moment.

McComb set his glass down. 'I hear you're having it out with Tate and his man O'Brien tomorrow.'

Wilson grunted. 'I see Rueda's mouth is a lot faster than his gun.'

McComb glanced at him. 'I come back because of Hank Logan. He wouldn't want this town to be taken over by troublemakers like the NPM.'

Wilson laughed in his throat and they all looked at him for a moment. Then Mallory turned to McComb. 'I didn't know you and Hank were that close.'

McComb sighed. 'I didn't either. Anyway, I want to be with you tomorrow. I got no reservations about Tate. I never did like that little fake marshal. He really started all of this. So now he'll have to deal with what it's become.'

Mallory was wearing a big grin. 'Why, that's just great, McComb! Jennings here has volunteered to stand with us, too. We'll have four guns out there.'

But Wilson wasn't smiling. He saw McComb as a competitor for power, when the confrontation was over. 'I told you, Mallory. We don't need all these guns. We only need mine.'

'You never know what you'll need,' McComb told him. 'Until the lead starts flying.'

Mallory gave Wilson a subservient look. 'Let's take all the help we can get, Wilson. What can it hurt?'

Wilson shrugged arrogantly. 'Fine. Just keep out of my way when it goes down.'

McComb studied Wilson's hard face. He had never liked him from the moment Mallory hired him. Neither him nor Rabbit Purcell. And he didn't think he would like a town run by Wilson. After the shoot-out, McComb decided, he would find a way to get rid of Wilson. And maybe help Mallory run the Dogie.

'We're all part of the original Peace Commission,' Mallory was saying to them. 'And that's good. We have to go out there tomorrow holding ourselves out as an alternative arm of the Sulphur Creek law. Challenging corruption and murder within the marshal's office. When this is over we'll need some kind of acceptance in this town. By our illustrious Mayor Provost, and even by the governor. We don't want it to look like anarchy here.'

Wilson studied Mallory's face closely. He didn't like Mallory trying to sound like he was running things. 'I don't give a damn what Provost thinks of us.'

Mallory felt the sudden hostility, and looked quickly around the table to note the reaction of the others. 'Well, I'm just saying it can't hurt to come out of this looking like a legitimate force here.

But I'll talk to Provost first thing afterwards. He's been with us so far in this.'

'Provost will take the side of them that win,' McComb commented.

'Pin Tate's badge on me, and I'll arrest the bastard if he gives us any trouble.' Jennings grinned. Mallory had suggested he might get the job.

They all regarded him with ill-hidden disdain.

'Right, Jennings,' Mallory said quietly.

'You won't have to do no talking to Provost or anyone,' Wilson said. 'You still don't seem to get it, Mallory. When this is over, we can appoint our own mayor.'

'Well of course,' Mallory said hesitantly. 'If it becomes necessary.'

'Success to the Peace Commission,' McComb said sourly, raising his glass.

Wilson swigged a shot-glass of rye down. 'That's guaranteed, McComb. I thought you knew that.'

Then the two of them sat staring

silently at each other, already recognizing a dangerous enmity in their potential future.

★ ★ ★

Over at the jail it was very quiet. It was getting to be late evening, but nobody was ready to try to find sleep. Jock was walking up and down the short corridor from front to back of the building, trying to build his stamina, as if he were going to be at the confrontation with Mallory.

Uriah Tate was sitting quietly at his desk, cleaning and oiling his Colt Navy revolver. He was very tense inside. He knew that he might not live past the big shoot-out, and that bothered him more than it would have before he undertook the care of Jock Sumner.

O'Brien showed no sign of concern. He had fried them some eggs earlier, and brewed some coffee. He went over to the gun case in the corridor as Tate was putting his Colt away. Jock was coming back down the corridor.

'I'll give you a nickel to quit marching up and down here, kid,' he said, smiling at Jock. 'I think you're making the marshal jumpy.'

'Oh. Sorry, O'Brien.'

Tate looked up, his face full of worry. 'Hell, it's OK. It's just the waiting to hear from them that worries a man's belly.'

O'Brien unlocked the case as Jock sat on a chair near Tate. 'It's time to break out these shotguns. Make sure they're clean and loaded.' He took one out and examined it. 'We'll take these Remington double-barrels. The singles would be no good.'

'You don't want sidearms?' Tate asked him.

'The eight-gauges got about the same range, and you don't have to be as accurate,' O'Brien reminded him. 'You don't need to get into no fast-draw contest out there. This ain't no game we're playing. And I'd guess you ain't as fast or accurate as Wilson with that Colt, Uriah.'

Tate grinned weakly. 'No, you're right. Even with the scatterguns we might not get a shot off against Wilson.'

Jock swallowed hard and felt a dampness in the palms of his hands. 'What about your Winchester?' he said to O'Brien.

O'Brien shook his shaggy head. His beard was full now and, bare-headed, he looked very primitive. He sat down on the remaining straight chair and began oiling the Remington. 'That won't work. They won't come out of the Schooner till they make sure we ain't carrying rifles. If we did, they'd make it a game of ambush. Nobody wants that.'

Jock was always surprised by O'Brien's acumen with guns and their use. 'Shotguns against Wilson's Enfield Mark II. It's well-balanced and accurate. I don't like it, O'Brien.'

O'Brien smiled at him. 'Would you try to relax, kid? We ain't lost this war yet.' He threw the oiled shotgun over the desk to Tate. 'Here. I'll get another one. Try to find some dry cartridges for them.' As he turned to the gun case again, a loud knocking came at the locked front door.

O'Brien turned back to the door and Tate drew his Colt. They exchanged a questioning look. O'Brien nodded to him.

'Who's out there?' Tate yelled out.

'It's Avery Hawkins!' came the muffled response. 'Let me in!'

O'Brien nodded again. Tate went to the door and opened it. Hawkins came in quickly, and Tate relocked the door behind him. Hawkins was breathless.

'Have you been out lately?'

'What the hell do you want, Avery?' Tate said impatiently.

'Mallory recruited Jennings from the Dogie to stand with them,' Hawkins said excitedly. 'And an hour or so ago, Maynard McComb rode in and went directly to the Schooner.'

O'Brien and Tate exchanged looks.

'Oh, hell,' Jock muttered.

'There will be four of them,' Hawkins went on. 'Against just you two.'

'We can do the math, Avery,' Tate said, slumping on his chair.

O'Brien shrugged. 'It's still Wilson.'

'If he doesn't get it done, there's three others,' Hawkins explained, as if they didn't understand.

'Why does that mean anything to you?' O'Brien said casually. 'You started this whole damn thing.'

Hawkins lowered his eyes. 'I know. Sometimes I wish we'd stayed in Kansas City. This is worse than the Dodge City war. And we know what the situation will be if Mallory takes charge of this town. Him and that Wilson. So I came here to help, Marshal. I'm going to stand with you when this happens. Everybody thinks it will be tomorrow. I'll be there beside you.'

'What?' Tate said.

Hawkins put his hand over an old revolver on his hip. 'I can shoot. I haven't used this thing in a while, but I used to be pretty good. It will give you three guns against four.'

'It will give Wilson one more man to murder,' O'Brien said, taking a second shotgun from the case. 'Forget it.'

Hawkins looked over quickly at Tate, who was regarding O'Brien pensively.

'Does he speak for you, Marshal?' Hawkins said.

Tate turned to Hawkins. 'I treat O'Brien like a deputy, Avery,' he said. 'And I listen when he talks. Have you given this a lot of thought?'

'I told you. I don't want to be in a town run by Wilson and Mallory. And O'Brien is right. We did sort of start this. I want a chance to redeem us in the eyes of the town.' He turned to O'Brien. 'Do you want to deprive me of that remnant of dignity?'

O'Brien turned to him, holding a second shotgun now. He aimed it at Hawkins's belly. 'You ever had a gun aimed at you to kill you, Hawkins?' he said levelly.

Hawkins felt a tingle of fear race through him, looking down the two barrels of that long gun. He swallowed.

'No. I haven't. But I'm up to it.'

'Can you use a shotgun?'

A nervous grin. 'I guess I'd prefer my revolver.'

'You mind standing a minute, Uriah?' O'Brien asked him.

Tate eyed him quizzically, but Jock knew what was coming. Tate rose from his chair.

'Now draw down on him.'

Now both Tate and Hawkins gave him a questioning stare.

'Let's see his reaction to it,' O'Brien explained.

Tate sighed. 'Oh, hell. You ready, Hawkins?'

Hawkins turned fully to Tate. 'Well . . . I guess.'

Tate drew his Colt in a rather fast draw and Hawkins went clumsily for the old revolver on his hip. It was out a full two seconds after Tate's gun was aimed at his chest. Hawkins looked embarrassed.

'I can probably do better than that.'

'Wilson is four times that fast,'

O'Brien said flatly. 'Sorry, Uriah. But it's true.'

Tate holstered his Colt, and Hawkins sheepishly followed suit.

'I'll practice tonight,' Hawkins said.

The way he said it got to Tate. 'It's all right, Avery. You're in.' He looked over at O'Brien. 'What the hell, Uriah.'

'It's OK, O'Brien.' Jock finally spoke up, softly. 'He's earned the right.'

O'Brien's face relaxed. After a moment he nodded. 'OK. You're in. You sure you don't want an eight-gauge?'

'I think I'd be less nervous with this,' Hawkins said.

O'Brien let out a deep breath. 'Well, you can go out there with it holstered or in hand. On one hand, you're fair game as soon as you hit the street, and from any gun. On the other hand, you can't even beat Jennings in a draw-down. It's your choice.'

Hawkins looked down at his gun. 'I'll think on it.'

'In the meantime, you stay here at the jail with us,' O'Brien told him. 'This will probably happen tomorrow. Did you say your goodbyes to anybody?'

A weighty silence filled the small room.

'No. I didn't think of it. Maybe I should go see Ned Tanner. I didn't give him any instructions. He'd be the chairman.'

O'Brien shook his head. 'I'd advise against that. Now that you made this trip down here, you'd be fair game. Go pick out a bunk back there. We still got some coffee here, too.'

'Thanks, O'Brien.'

'Let's hope you still feel that way tomorrow,' O'Brien told him. He started to add something about Hawkins's bedding when another knocking sounded at their door.

'This is getting to be like a damn circus tent!' O'Brien said irritably.

Tate and Jock looked very tense again. 'Who is it?' Jock called out.

'It's Mallory's barman! You know, Suggs!' the answer came back. 'I'm here under a white flag!'

O'Brien loaded a cartridge into the gun he held. Tate rose and drew his Colt from its holster. Taking a deep breath, he went and unlocked the door and carefully opened it. Mallory's obese bartender stood there, holding a white bar-cloth and sweating.

'I ain't armed! I got a message for you from Mallory.'

Tate looked around behind him. 'OK. Step inside.'

The barkeep came in, looking the room over. His gaze fell on Hawkins. 'Well. What do you know.'

O'Brien moved into the office area, and Suggs stumbled backwards a step. 'You're the hunter. You ain't going to shoot me, are you?'

'What's the message?' O'Brien said impatiently.

'Mallory says they'll meet you out on the street. In front of the Schooner. An hour after sunrise tomorrow. Winner take all. That's the way he said it.'

'You bastards!' Jock spat out.

'I ain't no part of it. I'm just

reporting. The Schooner won't be open tomorrow. He says there won't be no ambush. Just an open facedown. I'll be home, of course.'

'Hoping these men are all murdered in the street!' Jock cried out.

'It's all right, boy,' Tate told him.

'And now that you've delivered your message,' O'Brien said in an even tone, 'you can run back to that mud-hole you crawled out of and tell them we'll be there.'

'Yes, sir.' The barkeep nodded. He hesitated. 'There's four of them now, you know.'

'We know,' Tate said.

'Just remember I mentioned it. You know. If you get real lucky tomorrow.' A nervous grin.

'Get out, Suggs,' Tate barked out.

When he was gone Avery Hawkins found his tongue. 'That man has a lot of brass.'

'He's the same as the others,' Jock commented. 'But with no guts.'

'He doesn't give us a chance, does

he?' Hawkins said.

'And you take notice of what a weasel thinks?' O'Brien said caustically. 'Come on. Let's get you some bedding.'

They got Hawkins settled into the last available cell within a half-hour, then O'Brien finished loading the double-barreled Remingtons. Tate found some fresh .32 calibre cartridges for Hawkins's old Colt Army revolver. After that they sat around the office for a brief time, drinking coffee and making small talk while O'Brien busied himself with locking up the gun case for the night and stoking the fire in the small stove. O'Brien never actually sat down and talked to people. He found talk boring. Eventually, when it was getting time to find some rest, he came and spoke to them.

'We'll want someone awake through the night. I'll take first watch, Uriah. Jock will sleep through.'

Tate nodded. Jock wanted to protest, but knew it was pointless to argue with O'Brien, and he rather liked that. 'If you say so,' he agreed.

Hawkins and Tate both went to bed expecting not to sleep, but they eventually did. O'Brien sat up front at Tate's desk, a shotgun laid across the corner of it. He had had to sit awake countless times on the buffalo trail, for various reasons. The expectation of a big herd coming through in the dark; to ward off coyotes or wolves from his fresh kills; or with the knowledge that there were outlaws in the vicinity. Once, on a big buffalo hunt, he had stayed awake for four days and nights, tracking the herd as it moved, and protecting his skins. Now the day of the big herds and big hunts was gone. Now it was down to small-game hunting, and trapping, and it would be that way forever now, he realized. But at least that would keep him out on the trail, which was where he liked to be.

Two hours into O'Brien's three-hour shift he heard a sound from one of the cells back there. A moment later Jock came down the short corridor and sat down near him. He was somber-faced.

'I woke up,' he said, adjusting the bandage under his shirt. 'I've got tomorrow in my head now.'

'It's just past midnight,' O'Brien told him. 'You got a lot of hours ahead of you, kid.' He went over to Jock and opened his shirt, examining the thick bandage. 'The wound has stopped weeping into your bandage. You're healing real good.'

Jock nodded. 'The doc will be pleased.'

'You'll be riding in another week. You're just as tough as your uncle.'

That put a smile on Jock's face. But it dissolved quickly. 'O'Brien. What do you really think about tomorrow?'

O'Brien sighed. 'You got to clear your head of that, Jock.'

'I can't.'

O'Brien went back to the desk and sat down again. 'I reckon a racetrack better would put money down against us. But I never spent much time worrying over odds.'

'What do you think about Wilson?'

'Oh, Wilson. I think Wilson made a mistake, calling me out.'

Jock smiled through his worry. That was the kind of answer he had hoped for. And expected. 'O'Brien?'

'I'm still here, kid.'

'When we were out there hunting together . . .'

'Yeah?'

'You never really told me why you wouldn't shoot that last buffalo.'

O'Brien stared past Jock for a moment. 'I reckon there's a few reasons. But maybe mostly because he reminded me of me.'

Jock regarded his friend soberly. 'You will be careful out there tomorrow?'

'I ain't known for careful.'

'We're depending on you.' But as soon as he said it he was sorry. After a long silence between them, he said, 'Forget I said that.'

O'Brien smiled at him. It was different from his world; being confronted every day with such innocence.

'I know how important it is,' he said simply. He leaned forward on his chair. 'Look, Jock. I have no worries about tomorrow. But if something should go wrong, and you was left alone, what about that ranch where you worked? Would they take you back?'

Jock shrugged. 'I suppose so. They liked me out there.'

O'Brien nodded. 'If Wilson took over this town, it wouldn't be safe for you here. I want you to ride out there and take up with them again. You'll be ready for light work in a couple weeks. Will you do that?'

'I'd rather ride with you.'

'We been through that, kid.'

Jock nodded. 'OK. I will.'

'Good. Now maybe you should hit that cot again.'

Jock didn't move. 'O'Brien. I still don't know how Uncle Wesley died. You just said he was shot.'

'I don't talk about that stuff,' O'Brien said.

'I'd sure appreciate it,' Jock persisted.

'It's kind of important to me.'

O'Brien clasped his thick hands in front of him. He had done more talking with this boy than he had with other folks in the past year. 'I'll say this once. Then don't never ask me again.'

'I wouldn't.'

'Certainty Sumner and me was after the Gabriel gang, riding together. He was after bounties, and I had a score to settle with them. They ambushed us on the trail, from behind rocks. I never miss stuff like that. But I did. We didn't even get our guns clear. Sumner was hit twice in the chest, and me once. While we was down, they shot Sumner again in the head, and me in the chest, and left us for dead. Travelers found us and buried Sumner. He was finished after the head shot. They was burying me when I moaned once. They turned me over to an old man who nursed me back. And that's all of it.'

He had said it all in a matter-of-fact tone, as if recalling a turkey hunt.

'You're what's left of Sumner,' he

added after a while, looking over at Jock. 'That's why you have to take care of yourself.'

'I'm glad you told me that,' Jock said quietly. 'If they'd buried you that day, I wouldn't have been writing to you, and you wouldn't be here to save Sulphur Creek from Mallory and Wilson.'

'Take it easy, kid. I ain't saved nobody from nothing yet. Like I said before, you better go try to get some shut-eye. We're going to have a big day tomorrow.'

'I'm real proud to know you, O'Brien.'

'Go on to bed now,' O'Brien said softly. 'We don't need two of us up here watching for spooks. I'll see you in the morning.'

A moment later he was alone with his thoughts.

11

The sun rose the next morning at exactly eight minutes after six.

The eastern sky turned from black to a deep mauve so gradually that the eye could not capture when the subtle change occurred. Then there was a brief period when blood-red pencil lines of clouds streaked the burgeoning horizon, followed by the spectacular appearance of the peach-hued orb itself, just a sliver of color at first, but then revealing its full splendor to the expectant world of Sulphur Creek.

Those who waited for its arrival at the jail had been up long before that dramatic announcement of the new day, though. O'Brien had been awake since just after four, when he joined Hawkins who had taken the last watch. Everybody was up by five, and drinking coffee quietly in the marshal's office, each one dealing with the coming showdown in his own way, and privately.

O'Brien had made a last-minute check of the two shotguns they intended to carry into the fray. Hawkins checked and rechecked the ammunition in his Colt, looking and acting very nervous. Jock said little, but O'Brien noticed he was breathing shallowly the entire time. Tate tried to avoid the boy's eyes, for fear Jock would see the raw terror in them. He well knew how important it was for Jock that they prevail soon, out on the morning street.

'Anybody want eggs?' O'Brien offered at 6:30. 'There's still time if you're hungry.' He had had a couple raw an hour earlier.

Nobody accepted the offer. Their minds were not on food. O'Brien walked back to the cells and made up his cot, busying himself with small tasks as if nothing was about to happen. At ten to seven he returned to the office up front. They all looked tense.

'Is everybody ready?' he asked casually.

Tate nodded tightly. 'I reckon so.'

Hawkins tried to answer, but his mouth was too dry.

'Will they be out there waiting?' Jock asked hollowly.

'I expect they'll wait till they see us on the street,' Tate said. 'You stay put, Jock. I don't want you hit with a stray bullet.'

'I'm going out there,' Jock said defiantly. 'I want to see it.'

'You stay to hell here!' Tate yelled at him.

'Uriah,' came O'Brien's calm voice. 'Let him watch it go down. He ain't armed, and they know that.'

Tate's face relaxed a bit. 'Well. You can see everything from the hotel. You can walk that far with us. Just keep well out of the way.'

'It's almost seven,' O'Brien said. 'We better get out there.'

They left the marshal's office a couple of minutes later. Hawkins was so tightly wound he could barely walk. It was a beautiful spring morning, but there wasn't a soul on the streets. The entire town knew what was going to happen out there. In the immediate area a few individuals were peeking out of windows and cracked-open doors, especially at the Frontier Hotel, which was situated across the street from the Prairie Schooner, and a bit closer to the jail. Jock left them at the hotel, leaning against a canopy post and feeling his healing wound a little. Then the three of them walked abreast up the street, with O'Brien in the center. The shotguns were held loosely under their arms, and Hawkins kept his gun hand close to his old revolver. At that moment, he felt foolish for volunteering for such a thing.

Down the street fifty yards, just inside the swinging doors of the closed-down saloon, McComb squinted at the approaching trio.

'There they are,' he reported to those standing behind him. 'They got Hawkins with them. Just like Suggs said.'

Wilson moved up beside him, and studied the scene. The three men on the street had stopped thirty yards away. 'They've got shotguns,' Wilson grinned. 'My God, I can load that buffalo man with lead while he's hefting the muzzle of that thing.'

'Shotguns?' Mallory said, coming up to the doors. Jennings hung back, not really wanting to see. 'I hate shotguns. They scare me.'

'Everything scares you.' Wilson scowled at him. 'Don't worry, I'll take the hunter down first. Tate probably can't even use that thing. Let's go do it.'

Jennings slid his Wells Fargo revolver in and out of his holster a couple of times, feeling much like Hawkins on the other side. Maybe falling in with Mallory wasn't such a great idea, considering the risk. He had felt much better when it was four to two.

A moment later Wilson stepped out onto the porch of the Schooner, with the others close behind him. Down the street a short distance, their adversaries watched as the four men came down into the street, and lined up four abreast, facing the threesome representing the law.

'Hold it right there!' Tate called out. He didn't want their sidearms any closer.

Wilson was feeling very confident. 'What's the matter, Marshal? You aren't afraid of these little sidearms, are you? With those big, heavy weapons of yours.'

Tate ignored him. 'I hope you realize what you're doing here, Mallory,' he went on. 'This is an assault on the office of marshal. An attack on the established law here. You won't have the town with you in this.'

'You let us worry about the citizens of Sulphur Creek,' Mallory said, his mouth dry.

'Yeah. After you're gone.' Wilson grinned.

O'Brien was watching Wilson closely, assessing his body size, and his lithe build. He particularly paid attention to Wilson's eyes as he spoke.

Over on the hotel porch Jock had almost stopped breathing. Waiting for it to happen. Hoping his universe didn't explode in his face.

'I'm giving you a last chance to come to your senses,' Tate added. 'All four of you are under arrest for conspiracy to murder. Come peaceably and I'll see that you get a fair trial.'

Wilson laughed out loud, enjoying this brief preliminary.

'You talk about murder, damn you?' McComb shouted angrily at them. 'While you stand beside the murderer of Hank Logan! What do you say to that, O'Brien?'

'I say quit running off at the mouth and get on with what you come out here for,' O'Brien said in a deep, menacing voice.

'Jesus!' Hawkins whispered.

Wilson's face went taut after that

response of O'Brien, and he cast a quick glance at Mallory to indicate he was ready. Then a tight, chest-clenching silence that seemed like eternity filled the street.

'We're not murderers, Marshal,' Mallory called out. 'I'm giving you fair warning. Defend yourselves!'

Behind Tate's group, on the hotel porch, Jock's dry mouth tasted like old paper. Tate's eyes swept the line-up of four gunmen, but O'Brien's focus was on Wilson. He had learned something early on in confrontations, with men or wild beasts. You didn't watch for the first physical movement to signal an attack. You watched your adversary's eyes. There was almost always a subtle change of expression in the eyes before it happened, and that was especially true in men. In those few breathless moments when time stood still, he was watching Wilson's hard eyes. If a man's vision was good enough and he watched very carefully, he could always tell when a gunslinger was about to act.

Those thoughts had just run through O'Brien's head when he saw the almost imperceptible, deadly squint in Wilson's eyes. In the next split second, and faster than anyone there could follow, he drew the widow-maker Enfield and fired it twice. The explosions ripped through the still morning air like twin lightning bolts.

But when O'Brien saw Wilson's almost indiscernible change of expression, he had started a drop into a half-crouch, a movement down and to his right. In that same second, hot lead grazed O'Brien's left ribcage and his neck, missing his jugular by a half-inch. Almost at the same instant, McComb's Wells Fargo barked out so close to Wilson's shots that the three sounded almost as one roaring eruption. That lead tore a long hole in O'Brien's left sleeve, tugging at him as it passed through.

O'Brien's eight-gauge was raised now as Wilson, not quite as calm, fired off a third round that missed O'Brien's right ear and almost hit Jock on the hotel porch. At that same moment O'Brien squeezed off a round of the shotgun, and hit Wilson in mid-torso, almost cutting him in half.

While Wilson flew off his feet, Mallory fired and struck Tate in the left shoulder, staggering him for a moment. His shotgun roared out as he staggered backward, and struck McComb in the left arm, shredding it and spinning him off his feet, just as Wilson hit the ground near him. Jennings then fired and hit Hawkins in the top of the right thigh, but Hawkins was able to return fire and hit Luke Mallory in the belly. Mallory also flew to the ground, as Tate aimed for the first time and fired off the second barrel of the eight-gauge. He hit Jennings in the groin and legs, putting him down screaming.

Wilson, torn in half, tried to rise up far enough to fire at O'Brien a last time, and while that caught O'Brien's attention, McComb, with his destroyed left arm, sat up more successfully and aimed again at O'Brien. Wilson's shot fired into the air, and he fell dead. Then Jock's voice cried out from the porch.

'O'Brien! McComb!'

O'Brien whirled and fired the shotgun a second time, and beat McComb, hitting him in the head and blowing the side of his face off. He fell heavily onto his back, and for good.

The air was so thick with gunsmoke that Jock could taste it in his mouth.

Jennings had quit yelling. He, Wilson and McComb lay dead in the street. Uriah Tate was up and holding his shoulder. Mallory was lying in the dirt, his hand over his abdomen, looking pale-faced and stunned. Hawkins was grabbing at his shot leg.

It was over.

The whole thing had taken less than thirty seconds.

Up on the porch, Jock whistled between his teeth. 'Holy Jesus!' he whispered.

O'Brien walked over to the corpses of Wilson and McComb. He had just been nicked a couple of times, and the lead had barely drawn blood. He stood over Wilson for a moment and shook his head. 'Where did fast get you, you goddam snake?'

'Help me!' Mallory was choking out. 'Don't let me die in the street!'

Tate went and bent over him, feeling dizzy from his wound. 'You ain't hit bad, you bastard. The doc will fix you up just in time for you to stand trial.' A lone citizen had emerged from the hotel, and came out onto the street with Jock. 'You,' Tate yelled at him. 'Go get the doc.'

Jock came up beside them then. 'By God, you're good!' he said to O'Brien.

O'Brien turned to him. 'Appreciate the call-out,' he said. 'That weasel might've got one in me before I killed him.'

Jock smiled. 'Probably not.' He walked over to Tate and O'Brien followed.

'You're hurt,' Jock said, examining Tate's shoulder.

301

'It's a through and through,' Tate said. 'The doc will give me a sling and I'll be back to work tomorrow.' He turned to O'Brien. 'We owe you, mister. We'd be lying in the street now without you. You took Wilson down. To be honest, I didn't think it could be done.'

'Neither did Wilson,' O'Brien said. 'That's why he's lying there instead of me. Now let's get your shoulder fixed up. You look a little light-headed.'

'Are you OK?' Tate asked him.

'OK? Hell, I'm so hungry I could eat my horse.'

Jock and Tate exchanged a small smile, as Dr Scott was seen hurrying down the street toward the bloody scene.

In the next hour, Mallory was taken to the doctor's house on a stretcher, and given a sedative for later surgery.

'There isn't much bleeding. I think he'll be fine,' the doctor told them.

While still awake, Mallory rambled on about keeping the Schooner open, and some relative who would do that for him. The lead was pulled out of Hawkins's thigh even before Mallory was unconscious, then Tate's shoulder wound was cleansed and heavily bandaged, and his left arm was placed in a sling. The doctor wanted him to stay there overnight, but Tate took a swig of laudanum and left with Jock and O'Brien. Tate thanked Hawkins for his help, and Hawkins limped down the street toward Nell Douglas and Ned Tanner, who had come out to meet him, looking terrified.

O'Brien, Jock and Tate went over to the hotel past a new crowd of sober-faced citizens, many of whom called out congratulatory remarks to them. The corpses of the three dead gunmen had already been collected by the undertaker, but there were dark stains on the street where the action had taken place. O'Brien passed them without a glance.

At the hotel, O'Brien ate a steak while Jock and Tate had lighter fare. Tate didn't finish his stew, and was feeling the shoulder despite the laudanum. Jock was feeling oddly exhilarated, and tried to hide it. There wasn't much talking at the table, and when they were finished eating they sat in silence for a long time.

At last it was Uriah Tate who spoke. 'The guns are gone from Sulphur Creek. It's crazy, but I can't get my head to believe it's over. After living with it like we did.'

'Wilson's ghost might haunt this place for quite a spell,' O'Brien said with a smile. 'Let it be a lesson to these people.'

'The NPM finally got what it wanted,' Jock mused. 'The saloons are both closed down. At least for now. Hawkins will be a hero with them. Maybe he'll run for mayor against Provost next fall.'

'I'd vote for him,' O'Brien said. 'He had guts, going out there. But I hope he's smart enough not to go against reopening the saloons. Most folks need them. Just like you need that laudanum right now.'

They both studied his face, and realized at the same time that he felt what had happened out there on the street was not just a victory, but also a failure of sorts.

'What's next for you, O'Brien?' Tate asked him soberly.

'Oh, I'm leaving,' O'Brien said, swigging some cold coffee from a heavy cup. 'I'll be riding out about dawn tomorrow.'

Jock had pushed that reality into the back of his head, and was momentarily shocked by the announcement. 'Tomorrow! Why, isn't that a little soon? I was counting on some quiet time for us. I'd love to get in one more bird shoot. We could have a kind of farewell supper. Just the three of us. There isn't time today.'

O'Brien regarded him warmly. 'You knew this was temporary, Jock. I'd've been long gone if it wasn't for Wilson. You'll be fine. You done yourself proud, boy.'

They didn't talk about the deadly

showdown or O'Brien's departure again during the rest of that day. Tate and Jock took a well-needed rest on their cots until supper time, while O'Brien spent some time at the hostelry, getting his gear and the Appaloosa ready for an early morning departure. The horse could sense what was happening, and was very excitable.

The evening was spent quietly, with Jock and Uriah playing cards for a while, and Jock sneaking looks at O'Brien, who was cleaning and oiling his Winchester rifle over against the wall, bare-headed, dark hair slicked back, looking ruggedly handsome in his full beard. Earlier he had sewn up the rip in his tunic sleeve from McComb's near miss. As Tate gathered up cards on his desk and prepared to shuffle again, O'Brien looked up and spoke to him.

'You better hire yourself a deputy now, Uriah,' he suggested. 'You won't be fit for a while.'

'I won't have to be, thanks to you,' Tate replied. 'No, I'll limp along like this till I'm healed.'

O'Brien laid the Winchester aside. 'Jock will be sixteen pretty soon this year, won't he?'

Tate looked over at him. 'Yes. That's right.'

'Why don't you give him a birthday present he'll remember?' O'Brien suggested. 'Pin a badge on him. The boy has been itching for that a while, and I reckon he's proved he's ready to handle it. There won't be no big trouble in town for some time now. It would be a perfect time to break in a new deputy.'

Jock's face had grown flushed with excitement through that summary. He smiled widely at O'Brien, and then turned to Tate, who was somber-faced.

'Well. I just don't know. I was going to offer it to him. But in another year.'

'This boy has growed up a few years in the past weeks,' O'Brien countered. 'If I was wearing a badge here, I'd be pleased and proud to have him standing beside me.'

Jock turned and just stared at O'Brien.

Nothing he could ever hear from anyone could touch him more deeply. He could hardly speak. 'Thanks,' he mumbled, almost inaudibly.

Tate looked over at Jock and at last nodded his agreement. 'I think you're right. When summer comes, you'll be my new deputy, boy.'

Jock rose from his chair. Trying to hold his emotions in check, he said, 'Uriah, you'll never be sorry. I won't let you down.'

'I know that,' Tate told him.

Tate broke open a pint bottle of whiskey after that, and they all drank to Jock's sixteenth birthday.

The following morning O'Brien was up before dawn. He had been down to the hostelry and returned by the time Jock and Tate were up and moving about. They met him out in front of the jail then, and saw him off as he boarded the mottled stallion and prepared to leave.

'Did you put that slab of dried beef in your bag I made up for you?' Uriah

Tate asked him. He looked a bit older to O'Brien than he had on O'Brien's arrival in town.

O'Brien nodded. 'That will be my first meal on the trail.'

Jock was silent. This was a very emotional moment for him, and he didn't want to look like a child to O'Brien, at the last minute.

'The trail is easy south of here,' Tate was saying. 'You should have a good day of riding.'

O'Brien nodded, and looked down at Jock. He was feeling an emotion he hadn't felt since leaving the Shenandoah after the loss of his parents. 'Now you take care of yourself, kid. We're going to bag us some real birds my next time through here.'

Jock nodded, and at last felt safe to speak. 'Did you say you're headed for the Indian territory?'

O'Brien nodded. 'There's this hide man I know in a town southwest of here owes me money. I might stop there overnight, then I'm heading south. An old hunting partner of mine says there's good trapping down that way. If there is, I might be there awhile. I just follow the game, wherever it leads.'

Tate grinned. 'I almost wish I was going with you,' he said, not realizing how strongly Jock had expressed the same sentiment. 'You take care, buffalo man.'

O'Brien tipped his worn Stetson to him. 'You're a good man, Marshal.'

He turned a long, steady look on Jock then, before lightly spurring the stallion into motion. A moment later he was headed out of town toward an unknown and unknowable future, one that could be fraught with all kinds of harrowing dangers and adventure.

But that was the kind he had always openly embraced.

THE END

We do hope that you have enjoyed reading this large print book.

Did you know that all of our titles are available for purchase?

We publish a wide range of high quality large print books including:
Romances, Mysteries, Classics
General Fiction
Non Fiction and Westerns

Special interest titles available in large print are:
The Little Oxford Dictionary
Music Book, Song Book
Hymn Book, Service Book

Also available from us courtesy of Oxford University Press:
Young Readers' Dictionary
(large print edition)
Young Readers' Thesaurus
(large print edition)

For further information or a free brochure, please contact us at:
Ulverscroft Large Print Books Ltd.,
The Green, Bradgate Road, Anstey,
Leicester, LE7 7FU, England.
Tel: (00 44) **0116 236 4325**
Fax: (00 44) **0116 234 0205**

DEVINE

I. J. Parnham

Pinkerton detective Nimrod Dunn is hired by Lieutenant Governor Maddox Kingsley to infiltrate an outlaw gang. But when Nimrod's cover is blown, an innocent life is lost in the raging gun battle. The fearsome US Marshal Jake T. Devine then sets about bringing the outlaw Cornelius to justice — but his methods are as brutal as those whom he pursues. With Devine's blood-soaked trail making a mockery of the governor's promise to clean up the county, Maddox must call on Nimrod's services once more — to kill Marshal Devine . . .

HELL COME CALLING

Josh Lockwood

Big Jim Wolfe rides into the town of Greasewood for a rest, but instead finds himself defending a family of Mexican sheep-herders from a power-hungry cattle baron. Jack Whelan has the town under his control and is ready to launch an all-out bloodbath in order to gain the rest of the valley. But the one thing he hasn't counted on is the deep-seated sense of right and wrong that Jim Wolfe lives by. He isn't a man to go looking for trouble, but he certainly won't walk away from it . . .